LEADING HER TO HEAVEN

KAYLEIGH JAMISON

TEASE PUBLISHING

www.teasepublishingllc.com

This is a work of fiction. Names, characters, places, and incidents are products of the author's imagination or are used fictitiously and are not to be construed as real. Any resemblance to actual events, locales, organizations, or persons, living or dead, is entirely coincidental.

Leading Her to Heaven
A Tease Publishing Book/E book

Copyright© 2007 Kayleigh Jamison
ISBN: 987-1-934678-44-2
Cover Artist: Stella Price
Interior text design: Stacee Sierra

Tease Publishing LLC

PO BOX 234
Swansboro, North Carolina 28584-0234

For my grandfather, without whom I never would have discovered the haunting beauty of the Scottish Highlands, nor fallen in love with the history and culture of my ancestry. I miss you, Granddad.

And for the country of my origin, land of my heart, forever, Scotland the Brave.

Many thanks to:

Alisha Steele for her tireless editing and encouragement, and also for being a great friend.

Katrina Strauss, HS Kinn, Stella Price, Adra Steia, Skyler Grey, Cheri Valmont, Wendi Felter, and Cara North for being the fabulous group of women that you are, and making me work my ass off.

Emma Wildes for providing the wonderful title to this book. Darling, you are a great friend and an even greater writer. I can only hope to one day be as talented as you.

Sara, Jess, Lisa, and the rest of the Flo Co crew for keeping me sane in not always sunny Florida.

Chapter One

Lady Susanna Cavendish paced her antechamber like a tiger in the London Zoo. "I do not understand it," she said, her normally deep, contralto voice rising shrilly. "All my life he has told me they are barbarians who should be exterminated and now he gives my hand to one of them!"

Susanna's handmaid, Mary, clucked her tongue and continued packing the small trunk on the bed. "Ye know good an' well your father is as bothered by this as ye are, milady. Richard says he's visited the solicitor every day for a fortnight," she said in an attempt to placate her mistress. Richard was her brother, and the Earl's groom. "Weren't 'is idea, but the king's."

"Then I hate the king! Fat, mean old bastard!" Susanna hissed with such vehemence that Mary dropped the silk gown she'd been holding.

"Milady!" she exclaimed, with one hand over her mouth.

"My mother always told me that my marriage would be one of politics and not love, and I accepted that long ago," Lady Cavendish said. She shook her head with a sigh, curls trembling around her face, "but this is a fate worse than any I had imagined!" She blinked back her tears. She would not cry, she vowed silently. She was the eldest daughter of the Earl of Devonshire and she would not disgrace him by crying over her lot in life.

That didn't mean she wouldn't complain about it.

When she was a young girl, some amongst the peerage had expected Susanna to court the king himself, who was famous for keeping the most beautiful of the English ladies as his mistresses. Though she'd not been to court in years and her memories of the king were of a strikingly handsome, virile man, she'd heard that Henry was now fat and sickly. And given his penchant for finding ways to rid himself of his wives, Susanna was grateful she'd avoided catching the king's eye, after all. In fact, he'd seemed unaware of her existence entirely when she had reached marrying age, and he'd given no recommendation on a match.

Susanna had made excuses about her health to avoid going to court, in the hopes that Henry would continue to ignore her, allowing her to remain at her father's estate, in tranquil solitude, forever.

But three months ago, the Earl had been summoned to London and given the unsettling news. The king had found a husband for Lady Cavendish. It was, he'd said, a match that would benefit all of England. It was also not up for debate. Henry had affixed his own royal seal to the contract.

"It won't be so bad, milady," Mary said, putting a comforting arm around Susanna. "I'll bet he's 'andsome."

"He is a *Scot*!" Susanna exclaimed. "They are heathens who rape and beat their own women! Can you imagine what he shall do to an English lady?"

And her fiancé wasn't just any Scot, either. He was a Ruthven – a family of assassins with no moral code. The Ruthvens were one of the fiercest clans of Scotland; their cruel and violent nature considered to be worse, even, than their Highland brethren. Their hatred for the English was legendary. Lady Marveford's brother had been amongst the soldiers sent to Perthshire to negotiate with the Ruthven clan. He'd come back in a box, in pieces.

"How will I ever survive this, Mary?" Susanna lamented. She couldn't do this. Oh, dear Lord in heaven, she couldn't.

"Milady, ye'll be a Duchess." Mary's eyes always glazed over when she spoke of Susanna's new title. The comely girl pushed Susanna over to the mirror that hung on the far wall. "Just look at ye," she said, "the prettiest Duchess they've e'er seen, I wager."

Susanna sighed and looked at the girl – no, woman – in the mirror. Dark, green eyes, wide and slightly wet with unshed tears, stared back at her from behind her auburn locks. Her chin narrowed beneath her mouth, the lower lip full and pouty, giving her face a heart shape. Her cheekbones were high and naturally rosy against the porcelain of her skin. Pretty, yes, but a lot of good her looks had done her thus far. All noble women knew, from childhood, that they would never have the luxury of a happy union. But what young girl didn't dream of marrying for love? Of finding a husband who was kind, attentive, and accepting of who she was? Susanna would rather be nothing at all, if it meant she could stay in

Devonshire with her books and her drawings. "Mary, did you pack my books?" she asked, suddenly reminded of her favorite possessions.

"I packed a few, miss, but yer father was clear," Mary replied, returning to the task of packing. "Naught but a few can come, and only half yer paints."

"And that is the cruelest part of all this," Susanna sighed.

Mary gave her a hard stare. "Milady, ye need to stop pityin' yerself. The caravan comes at nonce, whether ye like it or no."

"I most assuredly do not like it, Mary," Susanna said sternly. She padded to her dressing table where a traveling gown was draped over the back of the chair. Snatching up the dress – made of coarse, gray wool, deliberately heavy and unglamorous, for hours of riding within the litter – she disappeared behind her wardrobe screen. "Mary?" she ventured, tossing her shift over the screen.

"Yes, ma'am?" Mary answered, evidently fretting over the small trunk in front of her, from the rustling Susanna could hear, growing more pronounced by the moment. Another sharp, snap of fabric almost caused her to peak around the dressing screen to investigate. The other servants had packed the other four trunks Susanna was allowed to take with her, but this one Mary was responsible for herself, and she was apparently having a devil of a time with it, too.

"Do you suppose he hates me already?" Susanna wondered aloud in a rare moment of honesty.

"I can't imagine 'e does, ma'am," Mary chirped. "'E did agree to marry ye, after all."

"But I thought they all hated the English," she mused, pulling her stockings on beneath her thin, white shift. She reached for the next layer of her clothing with a scowl. *Designed for comfort in travel, indeed,* she thought bitterly. *Comfort would be not wearing a corset at all!*

"'Aving not met one, milady, I can't say for sure," Mary interrupted her thoughts, "but I imagine yer beauty will stop 'im dead in 'is tracks."

Susanna sighed and surveyed the slender curve of her waist, running her hand along the dip of her hips. Her governess, Catherine, who had passed away just last year, had always told her she was too thin. *"Put some meat on yer bones, child, before ye waste away,"* she'd said on a daily basis.

"Knowing my luck," Susanna said sourly, "he prefers his women fat."

***

Blair Ruthven was experiencing something strange -- for him. He was nervous. Over a woman, of all things. Nerves before going into battle would be understandable, though Blair himself never had them, but nerves over a woman? It was downright embarrassing.

He paced the length of the great hall, back and forth, back and forth, like a caged beast. He hadn't bothered to unhook his sporran or his broadsword when he'd returned, and the accessories smacked against his thigh now as he stalked to and fro. The bright reds and greens of his mantle were a contrast to his tawny, sun-weathered skin, aqua-blue eyes, and unruly, brown hair. Four tight braids framed his strong, masculine face, while the rest of his long mane was left free, hanging down his back to just below his shoulder blades.

It had been three months since he'd signed the marriage contract, but the entire thing had seemed rather surreal to him until this morning, when the messenger had arrived with word that his bride to be would be leaving her father's estate and heading north within the week.

Blair had sent back that he would meet her in Edinburgh and accompany her the rest of the way to Perthshire, his family seat and her new home. Things were quiet for once; a begrudging peace of sorts had been reached between his clan and the Murrays to the south. And the Robertsons to the north were too damn scared of him to try anything foolish while he was gone. He could always send someone to meet his fiancée on his behalf – his brother, perhaps – but he preferred to go himself.

"I wager she's fat an' ugly," his younger brother announced, interrupting Blair's internal monologue. He was sitting at the end of the long dining table, one booted foot propped irreverently on the tabletop, a clay stein in his fist. "All English wenches are."

Blair sighed and ran a hand across the stubble of his beard. "I was promised she is'na fat."

Indeed, the messenger from the English king had come bearing a small portrait of the girl and, if the painting was accurate, she was the farthest thing from fat and ugly the Scottish Laird had ever seen. But he'd also heard stories of the king's crafty use of deception and trickery to get what he wanted. Still, he'd kept the tiny portrait; it sat in his bedchamber now. He hadn't shown it to anyone else, especially not his brother.

For some reason, he didn't want any other man to see her.

"Granted," his brother continued as if he hadn't spoken, "I do no mind some fat on my wenches, but for Henry not to want her, she must be dumpy in all the wrong places."

"Ceallach!" Blair exclaimed, using his brother's Gaelic name, as he often did when he was annoyed with him. Which was most of the time. "Ye speak of my future wife!"

"Aye, and it would'na do for ye to get yer hopes up, bràthair." Kelly took another swig of whiskey. "Why did ye ever agree to this?"

Blair sighed. He was tempted to grab the whiskey from his brother's hand and down it himself. Getting good and drunk, that would solve his problems. He couldn't remember the last time he'd been truly intoxicated. He wasn't sure, honestly, *why* he'd signed the marriage contract. James had been in favor of the match, but would not have forced him into it had he put up a fight, and Blair knew it. "The King thinks it will be good for Scotland," he said finally, the excuse sounding hollow even to his own ears. Good for Scotland -- right. When had a Ruthven ever given a damn about that?

"Aye, an' a nightmare for ye. Fat an' ugly, bràthair, mark my words."

**

"The caravan is here, milady." Richard's thick, accented voice interrupted Susanna's thoughts, startling her out of her reverie.

"Oh, please tell me you jest, Richard," she said with a sigh, looking up from the pages of the book she was reading.

"Milady," he said, but gentler this time, "What do ye read now?"

Her eyes lit up. She tilted her hands and held up the leather volume to show him the cover, forgetting for a moment that he could not read it. "*De vita et moribus sacerdotum opusculum*," she announced, her Latin fluid and smooth. "It is an exploration of the priesthood and the Reformation. Father brought it for me from London and it is simply fascinating."

"If ye say so," he replied, eyeing her suspiciously. Richard was of the opinion that the Earl overindulged his daughter by allowing her intellectual pursuits clearly meant for men of the nobility, and not women. His sister mentioned to him once, years ago, that she desired to ask Lady Susanna to teach her to read. Richard had laughed so hard he'd cried, and eventually Mary had abandoned the idea.

Susanna closed the book and took one final look around her small parlor. Was this truly the last time she would sit in her beloved window seat, looking out over the cultured grounds of her father's estate? Her heart ached at the thought.

Richard cleared his throat in a not-so-subtle attempt to hurry her along.

"All right, Richard, I take the hint," she said, standing and clutching the book to her breast.

Susanna followed her father's groom out of her chambers and down the narrow, spiral staircase to the great hall, where her father and his staff had gathered to see her off. Her gaze settled on the Devonshire coat of arms, carved into the stone above the fireplace.

Two stags, facing in opposite directions, one on its knees, the other standing, beneath the royal crown. Coiled above the crown, in an intricate figure eight, was a green snake. The family motto, *"Cavendo Tutus"*, covered the bottom of the crest. *Secure by caution.*

Susanna took a deep breath. *I am a Cavendish,* she told herself silently, repeating the words her father had taught her as a child. *There is honor in my name, and valor in my heart. With wisdom and truth I will secure my future and that of the Family.* She looked to her father who watched her nervously, as if he expected her to throw a public tantrum at any minute.

She didn't. And as much as she wanted to sweep past him without a word in parting, she knew she couldn't do that either.

"Richard," she said, loud enough for her father to hear, "I will be sending someone in two months' time to retrieve the remainder of my books. Please see that they are packed and ready."

Her father didn't bother to hide his condescending smile. Susanna knew that he believed she'd be lucky if the Scottish rake didn't throw all of her books into the fire the moment he saw them. Her father hid a smile. He thought his daughter should consider herself lucky if the Scottish rake didn't throw all of her books into the fire the minute he saw them.

Chapter Two

The litter jerked, tossing its occupants roughly against the wooden frame as it hit yet another rock-strewn hole in the road. Susanna groaned when her shoulder slammed against the side and sent a spark of pain through her arm.

"This," she said through clenched teeth, "is not the most pleasant journey I have ever had to endure."

"It's not so bad, milady," Mary said, rubbing her head where it had struck the top of the litter. A tall, lanky girl, she seemed even more uncomfortable than her charge, but was steadfastly keeping her mouth shut. Her place was to serve her lady, not to complain.

The Earl had provided them with a coachman, a handful of guards, and some newfangled contraption in which to travel – very similar to the litters used at court, the wooden box was carried by horses instead of men.

They were in their sixth day of travel, and Susanna was tired. The butterflies in her stomach had quelled temporarily, lulled by the discomfort of their journey, but as the caravan neared the Scottish border, some of her apprehension returned. They were well into Northumberland, and would likely cross into Scotland the following day. From there, it would only be two days or so until they reached Edinburgh, where Ruthven would be waiting for her.

Each night they sought refuge at the local inns. The proprietors were friendly enough, more than willing to provide food and shelter, as well as what meager comforts they could offer, for a price. Susanna willingly paid the inflated boarding prices. Anything was better than sleeping on the roadside or, even worse, in the litter.

The young Lady Cavendish was more grateful than ever for Mary's street smarts. She trusted the young handmaiden implicitly, allowing her companion to handle all negotiations for their accommodations and transportation. It wasn't that she thought herself better than the common folk, it was that she didn't know how to act or what to say.

As the Earl's eldest child and only daughter, Susanna's life had been decidedly sheltered thus far. When she'd been a child she had spent time in London, in the king's court at Whitehall. But following the death of her mother when she was twelve, Susanna had been allowed to become increasingly more reclusive. The Earl was an overindulgent, doting father who'd had children late in life. After losing his wife to the Sweate, he was more than happy to oblige his daughter's request to avoid attendance at court.

Susanna twisted in her seat to peer out through the curtains, just in time for the litter to pass over a large rock and send her face first into the wall.

"Damnation!"

"Milady!" Mary exclaimed. "What would yer father say if 'e heard that language?"

"My *father* is not here, Mary," Susanna said with a scowl, gingerly probing her forehead. "He is no doubt reading in his study before his evening meal, in a rather comfortable chair, or perhaps taking a quick rest." She scowled. "Either way, he is not being tossed around like day old fish in this awful contraption."

"Shall I inform the coachmen that milady wishes to walk?" Mary asked nonchalantly.

Susanna glowered at her. She again moved to look out the through the curtains, taking care this time to keep her head away from the wooden frame. The sun was beginning to set.

"Where are we, driver?" she called out.

"Northumberland's lands, milady," he shouted back to her. "Just south 'o the border with Scotland."

"Will we leave England before nightfall?"

"Nay. Be a good deal safer to rest 'ere tonight, milady. I've already sent 'enry ahead to secure lodgings fer the night."

"And how much farther to Edinburgh?" Susanna pressed.

"Well, I reckon we'll make it by tomorrow eve, milady."

She pulled her head back inside the litter and gave Mary a satisfied smile. Only one more day of this torture. Of course, once they reached Edinburgh she'd be introduced to her fiancé, and an entirely new form of torture would begin. But with any luck it would be less jarring.

One of the guards rode by and slowed to pace the litter. He looked both women over with unconcealed appreciation. Mary took notice and proceeded to silently flirt with him. Her charge, however, was lost in thought as she played out various future scenarios in her mind. Would he be kind to her? Would he let her keep her books? What did he look like? He was undoubtedly a brute and a heathen, but...

Susanna had never been a frivolous girl, and yet she thought that if her fiancé was handsome, perhaps it would not be so bad. She'd never seen a Scotsman. They lived outdoors, according to several papers she had read, preferring the elements.

When she was fifteen or so, her father had hired an Irishman to tend to the stables. He'd been rugged, and a bit crude, but quite good-looking. Though her father had offered the man living quarters in the manor, Andrew had declined, stating that his job was to tend the horses, and so he would sleep with them. Once, Susanna had -- on impulse -- kissed him on the cheek after he'd helped her dismount her mare. His skin had been hard, almost leathery from the sun, and when he'd cupped her cheek in response, his palm had been calloused and rough. Masculine. Despite herself, Susanna had enjoyed his touch, unrefined and dangerous, and had her sense of propriety not kicked in and caused her to run back to the manor house, she may have let him kiss her.

"Mary, do you think he is fat?" Susanna asked suddenly.

"No, I think 'e's rather 'andsome, milady," Mary replied, batting her eyelashes at the young soldier, who winked in return.

Susanna looked up and frowned. "I meant Lord Ruthven."

"Oh." The servant girl shrugged. "Aren't all old noblemen fat?"

Susanna's frown deepened. Her father was *not* fat. Merely... robust. "Ruthven is not old. My father said he is nine and twenty."

"Then no, 'e likely hasn't let 'imself go just yet," Mary replied jovially.

Susanna's attention was drawn away from her handmaid by the sound of children shouting. Peeking out the curtains, she saw several young boys – no older than seven or eight -- running alongside the litter, mouths agape in fascination.

"We must be near Newcastle upon Tyne," she commented, waving to the children and giving them a wan smile. Up ahead, she could indeed make out the massive walls of the city, England's northernmost stronghold.

"Haven't ye any food, lady?" one shouted. He was the smallest of the crowd, probably only about five.

"Shh!" another boy elbowed the first in the ribs.

"Oh. Mary..." Susanna began, looking about for something to give the boys. Of course they weren't interested in simply saying 'hello' to her.

"Here, milady," Mary produced a small bundle of sweetcakes, left over from their midday meal.

Susanna called to the driver to stop. She extended her hand and offered the bundle to the closest youngster, who snatched it away from her and pried open the cloth impatiently. The two ladies watched as he lifted one of the sweetcakes to his nose and sniffed. He cast a suspicious look at Susanna before darting his tongue out to lick the morsel.

His expression changed to one of satisfaction and he popped the entire cake into his mouth before handing the bundle off to another child.

"Are ye the Queen?" the youngest boy, the one who had asked for the food, inquired plainly. His accent was different from the one Susanna was used to, with a hint of the Scottish brogue to it.

"Ye fool!" another boy hissed at him. "The Queen is an ugly witch! She turns people to stone!"

"No, I am not the Queen," she replied with a smile.

The youngest cocked his head and thought for a moment. "Ye should be," he declared. "Ye are very fair an' bonny."

Susanna smiled and felt her cheeks flush at the compliment.

"Alright, on with ye, then," said the soldier who had been flirting with Mary earlier. "The lady must get into the city before dark."

"Aye," the boy nodded solemnly. "It is'na safe outside the walls. Be careful."

As the litter began to move again, Susanna called out, "What is your name?"

"Robert," he stated.

"It was nice to meet you, Robert," she replied.

The band of children huddled together and watched the small caravan ride through the gate. As the doors began to close, Susanna saw Robert lift his hand and wave.

Turning around to observe the city, she wrinkled her nose in disgust. Newcastle was not going to be the most pleasant of places if her assaulted sense of smell was any indication. The cobbled streets were coated with the stained slickness of urine and rotten food.

They passed through a stone archway which, Susanna noticed, was actually a large building. Windows flanked either side of the arch, and a large, multi-paned window spanned the top. Above that, the building rose for several stories.

"The castle," she murmured. "It must be."

"We won't be staying there, milady?" Mary asked.

Susanna shook her head. "Northumberland is in London getting married. There is likely very little staff inside at the moment."

" 'E's fat, isn't 'e? An' old?"

"Mary, hush. He is in his forties."

"And 'ow old is the bride?" the serving girl pressed.

Susanna sighed. Anna Spears was the same age as she. "Nineteen."

"Milady." Henry, the guard who had ridden ahead, materialized to walk beside the carriage. He must have been waiting just inside the gate for their arrival. "I've secured lodgings for ye. There is room at the inn or, if ye prefer, a Lord Spencer has offered use of 'is home."

Susanna thought for a moment. She didn't recognize the name. "Who is Lord Spencer?" she asked politely.

"Says e's a friend o' your father's, milady."

"I am sure Lord Spencer is a fine gentleman, Henry, but I am not familiar with him myself, and I think it best if we stay at the inn, if you please."

"As ye wish, milady."

The entourage made several turns before arriving at the inn. Henry helped each lady from the litter in turn, before escorting them inside.

The coachman hid a sneer as he watched the two women pick their way through the mud-caked street to the door of the inn. He had nothing personal against the Lady. She had, in fact, been almost kind to him throughout their journey, but he had a deep-rooted hatred for the nobility that prevented him from liking her, and more importantly, from feeling sorry for her.

No doubt she'd have the whole of England feeling sorry for her very soon.

The Earl of Devon's first mistake had been hiring someone with no loyalties to him to transport his eldest daughter from southern England all the way to Scotland. His second had been paying the man up front. And the Earl's third mistake had been how *much* he'd paid.

It had taken very little convincing on the part of the highwaymen he'd met earlier for the coachman to agree to their plan. The small band of thieves, led by a man who called himself Spencer, had approached him the night before and made an offer that he would have been a fool to refuse.

The coachman merely had to feign a problem with the horses and make a big show of trying to fix it. Then he was to send the guards off for help. When the thieves arrived, they would pay him double what his salary had been to turn a blind eye to whatever it was they chose to do with the noble woman and her maid.

Not that he couldn't guess what they planned to do. They'd spent a good part of the evening discussing the Lady Cavendish's 'assets'.

It didn't matter to him. Money was money. Wenches were wenches.

And, like any other starving commoner, he worked for the highest bidder.

***

"I do no care fer waitin'," Blair grumbled, speaking mostly to himself. The Duke of Perthshire was not accustomed to waiting for things. What he wanted, he took. And he'd never, *ever*, had to exert any effort to seduce a woman.

He was looking out over the interior courtyard of Holyrood Palace, where the king had granted him accommodations while he waited on the arrival of his bride. He'd arrived in Edinburgh earlier that day, and had been relieved, though at the same time displeased, that Lady Cavendish was not there.

His squire was moving about absently, tidying things that didn't need tidying. "Ah, yer Grace, she'll be here soon enough," said William. "That is, if she hasna run into trouble."

"Trouble?" Blair whirled around, the warrior in him suddenly alert. "What trouble?"

William shrugged. "I dinna ken, yer Grace. Only..." he trailed off as if suddenly unsure of the intelligence of his revelation.

"Only *what*?"

"Well, the king's pageboy was in the galley last night when I went to fetch yer dinner," the boy began, launching into one of his typically longwinded stories. "He goes often to the pubs in the city because the King wishes to hear the gossip an' his people are oft afraid to bring it to 'im directly. So he goes to listen an' then he tells the King what he 'ears."

"And?" Blair prompted, clenching his fists at his sides as he fought the urge to shake his squire.

"An' he said there's been trouble on the roads in Northumberland. Thievin' an' the like. He wasna sure why ye'd allow the Lady to travel such a dangerous way alone, an' I said that ye werena aware of the trouble."

"Indeed, I was no." Blair took a deep breath and rubbed a hand over his face while he considered his options. There weren't many. Even if she was fat and ugly, as his brother believed, it was his duty to keep her safe. He could hear his brother's voice in his head, *'God gave ye a way out of it and ye dinna jump at the offer, bràthair?'* "Ready my horse," he said finally. "I'm leaving."

"Leaving, milord? To go where?"

"To retrieve my bride."

Chapter Three

Susanna slept fitfully that night, tossing and turning on the stiff straw mattress. When she woke to the sound of the tavern mistress bustling about in the hallway and squawking at the serving boy, she was grateful for the reprieve. Dressing herself quietly, she left Mary to sleep while she crept downstairs. The room where they had lodged was rather stuffy and she wished for some fresh air, as well as the ability to move about and calm her restlessness.

She nodded to the tavern mistress, whom she passed at the foot of the stairs, and then wandered through the nearly empty dining hall to the entrance. As she drew closer to the door, she noticed one of her guards sitting in the corner, where he appeared to have stayed all night.

"Milady," Henry greeted her, standing.

"Henry, you did not sleep here, did you?" she asked.

"I thought it best, milady, to keep an eye on the door," he admitted. "It did not take long for word of yer presence in Newcastle to spread, an' I promised yer father I'd keep ye safe."

"I hope you allowed yourself some rest," Susanna said, her concern genuine.

"I slept a bit, milady," he replied. "Can I get ye anything?"

"Well, truthfully, I should like some fresh air. Might you escort me along the street for a bit?"

Henry lowered his voice. "I do not think ye will find fresh air in this city, madame."

Susanna laughed. "Perhaps not, Henry, but I wish to at least try."

"Then I am honored to accompany ye, milady."

He opened the door for her and she stepped out into the chilled, near morning. The cool air was soothing against Susanna's cheeks, but the stench of the city made it difficult for her to breathe comfortably.

Henry noticed her pained expression. "London has a very similar smell, milady."

"True, but I avoid London at all costs."

"Well, soon enough we'll be in Scotland, an' the air truly is fresher there," he said.

Susanna looked at him curiously. "You have been to Scotland, Henry?"

"I have, milady. Several times."

"But you are not dead," she said stupidly.

"I am not," Henry confirmed with a trace of amusement. "I thought it to be a beautiful place, in fact."

"And the people did not try to kill you for being English?"

"No, milady. On the whole I found them to be very friendly."

"Do you think they will hate me, Henry?"

"Anyone who would dare speak an unkind word to you, my Lady, is a fool," a voice interrupted before Henry could reply.

"I beg your pardon?" Susanna asked, turning to regard a tall, thin man standing several feet away, obscured by the fog and shadows of the predawn.

"Lady Susanna," the man tipped his hat and bowed. "I see a night at the inn did not agree with yer delicate sensibilities." He raked his eyes over her with a gaze that made Susanna immediately uncomfortable.

"Who might you be, sir?" she asked, swallowing her revulsion.

The man placed a hand over his heart. "It wounds me, milady, that ye do not remember me."

She was quite certain she'd never met this man before. "Indeed, sir, I do not believe we are acquainted."

"Lord Spencer, Madame." He reached for her hand and Susanna reluctantly produced it for him. He reeked of fish and grime and, though his clothes were refined, did not have the demeanor of a nobleman.

"I am afraid I cannot recall my father ever mentioning you, my Lord," she told him stiffly. "Tell me, how is it that you know my family?"

" 'Tis a rather long tale, indeed," Spencer answered smoothly. "I would be delighted to relay it if the lady would join me in breaking fast at my manor, just outside the city walls."

Her stomach churned. Something about this man was... wrong. "How very kind of you to offer, Lord Spencer," she said, "but I must be on my way early this morning if I am to reach my destination today. Therefore, I must graciously decline."

Spencer gave a small nod. "As my lady wishes," he said, before turning and heading down the alley.

"Henry," Susanna said, once Spencer had disappeared from sight. "I think I should like to go back inside now. I do not like that man."

"No, milady," Henry replied, with narrowed eyes still trained on the alley as if he expected the man to reappear. "Nor do I."

***

The caravan was prepared to leave just after sunrise. True to her word, Susanna planned for an early start so that they might arrive in Edinburgh that evening. It was better than another night on the road. Today, however, she chose to ride on horseback rather than inside the litter. She was quite tired of sitting in the contraption for one thing, and for another she was, despite her prejudices, rather curious to see the Scottish landscape. Henry's praise had eased her anxiety somewhat, and she decided to do her best to keep an open mind about the mysterious country that would be her new home.

She rode in the middle of the caravan, with Henry and the coachman in front of her, Mary at her side, and the three remaining guards at her back.

They had not traveled very far when the coachman held up his hand and brought them to a halt.

"What is it?" Mary called, glancing around.

The man dismounted and approached Susanna's horse. Taking hold of the reins, he studied the animal closely. "This horse is sick," he declared.

"He does not seem ill to me," Susanna protested.

"With respect, milady, 'e *is* sick an' if we keep going now, 'e's going to keel over with ye on 'is back."

"What shall we do, then?" she asked.

"Ye can ride my horse, milady," Mary offered. "An' I'll ride with the guards."

"I will walk," Henry said. "And give the Lady my horse."

The coachman shook his head. "Then we'll never reach Edinburgh before dark. Newcastle is still close by. Two of ye go back and see about purchasin' a new horse. We will wait here."

Henry considered for a moment. "I suppose that's a sound plan. I will stay with the women."

Two of the remaining guards offered to make the trek back to the walled city. They started off immediately.

***

The coachman watched the two guards ride out of sight, forcing himself to remain jovial and unassuming. The noble wench had inadvertently ruined his plan when she'd decided to ride on horseback, rather than in the litter. His lie about her horse's health had been a bad one, and he knew it.

Fortunately, the women had not argued with him. Now, all he had to do was distract them until Spencer arrived. And since one of the Lady's guards had been recruited into the scheme the night before, he would not have to control them all on his own if they did become suspicious.

Within moments of the two guards disappearing over the horizon, the coachman heard the steady rumble of horse's hooves approaching from the west.

"Who in the world...?" Susanna began, staring at the group of men as they drew closer. There were at least six of them, all on horseback. Only the leader was dressed respectably; the rest wore common rags.

"Perhaps they've come to offer help," Mary said, though the look on her face showed she didn't believe they had.

Susanna moved to spur her horse out of the path of the ruffian band whose pace had not slowed, but the coachman tightened his grip on the reins and held the horse still. Realization dawned, as at last she recognized the leader.

***

"Lord Spencer," Susanna said, her back rigid.

"Lady Cavendish," Spencer acknowledged, bringing his horse to a halt before her. "I have come to fetch ye to my home for the meal we spoke of earlier."

"And as I told you when we spoke, sir, I must decline your offer."

Spencer sneered. "But my Lady, I *insist*." He reached out and grabbed the reins of her horse.

"Stay away from her," Henry growled, drawing his sword.

"Ye have a very gallant escort, my Lady," Spencer remarked. "But, unfortunately, not a terribly bright one."

As he spoke, the other guard who had remained behind – the same one who had flirted with Mary the previous day – drew his sword. However, instead of turning back to back with his compatriot and preparing to defend his charge, he turned and thrust his sword deep into Henry's chest.

"No!" Mary cried.

Henry sputtered and glanced from the sword in his torso to Susanna. He opened his mouth to speak as he dropped to his knees. His own weapon struck the rocks of the road with a 'clang'.

The traitor turned to Mary and smiled. "Last night," he explained, "he promised that if I helped 'im with the Lady, I could have ye for miself."

Mary let out a choked sob. "Never in a thousand years," she said. One of Spencer's men grabbed a hold of her reins before she could think to flee.

"Now, my Lady," Spencer announced, "we return to my home. You," he nodded to the guard, "stay and see that this mess is removed from the road and hidden. Can't 'ave people gettin' suspicious. The little missy'll be waitin' for ye."

"And what about my payment?" the driver demanded. Susanna's heart sank. Him, too?

"Take what ye like from the Lady's things," Spencer instructed. "An' bring the rest to me."

***

Blair had ridden hard all night, slowing only when his horse tired to the point where it would have killed the animal to push it faster. By early morning, he was well into Northumberland, and though he stayed on the main road, he'd not found any trace of his bride's convoy.

The closer he drew to Newcastle, the more anxious he became. A nagging feeling in the pit of his stomach told him that something had happened to her. He began to wonder if the robbers had not pulled them off the road to avoid suspicion. What if he'd ridden past them already?

Just as he was prepared to backtrack and search alongside the road more thoroughly, he crested a hill and saw the evidence he'd been searching for – what was left of the caravan. Several horses were tied to trees nearby. A wagon was pulled to the side of the road and its contents strewn on the ground. A short, spindly man was bent over an open chest, rummaging through its contents. He was tossing dresses and hats into the dirt, with blatant disregard, as he searched for things of more value.

Two men were lying on the road, face down. One had obviously been run through with a sword. The other had a small dirk protruding from between his shoulder blades.

Blair slowed his horse to a stop and dismounted, wanting the element of surprise. Dropping into a crouch, he crept towards the unsuspecting thief's back.

He drew his broadsword and, within two long strides, he had him, one hand holding back the man's head by his hair, the other pressing the sword to his exposed neck.

"Where is she?" he growled into the man's ear.

"I don't know who yer talking about!"

"The Lady Cavendish," Blair said through gritted teeth. "Where is she?"

"I don't know any Lady!"

"No?" Blair jerked the man's head in the direction of a large trunk that lay open on the ground. The Earl of Devon's crest was carved into the wood, gilded in gold. "Then why do ye have her things?"

"Who are ye that I should tell ye anyway?"

"I," Blair hissed, "am Laird of the Ruthven clan. Do ye ken who we are?"

The coachman's eyes widened and he gave a slight nod of his head.

"I willna ask ye again."

"They paid me!" the man exclaimed, his voice rising to a squeak.

"Who paid ye, an' to do what?"

"To let 'im take 'er!"

"Where did he take her?" Blair pressed the blade harder against the man's neck, ignoring the trickle of blood that seeped around the edge of the steel.

"To a manor house not far from here! I was supposed to bring the belongings to 'im! I killed the one," he said, nodding to the man with the dirk in his back, "But 'e killed the other! Please!"

"Ye will take me there. Now."

***

It was a short ride from the site of their ambush to the manor house, which Spencer had clearly commandeered for his own devious purposes.

"You are no lord, and this is not your house!" Susanna cried, as he pulled her from her horse and carried her, slung over his shoulder, into the house.

"It is now, Madame," he replied with a sneer, one hand brazenly groping her uplifted rear. "The previous owner was reluctant to part with it, true, but there's naught 'e can say about it now, since 'e lies rotting in the garden out back."

"Northumberland will not stand for this!"

"He likely would not, if 'e were here," Spencer agreed, giving her ass a sharp smack. "But ye will have served yer purpose long before he returns, my Lady."

Once they were through the door he set her down, but kept a firm grip around her waist, holding her in place against his chest. Another man rushed forward and bolted the door.

"Take the money!" she said. "Take all of it and we will not complain, nor put up a fight!"

He laughed. "If I wanted yer money, pretty thing, ye'd be dead already. It's yer charms that interest me."

Mary, who had been carried into the house in similar fashion by one of Spencer's men, let out a shriek and grabbed hold of her captor's hair, yanking out a large clump. The man cursed and dropped her, one hand going to his head.

The handmaid turned and tried to rush at Spencer, but her assailant regained his senses and reached for her again. He grabbed Mary from behind, wrapping an arm around her neck. She promptly lowered her head and bit him as hard as she could, sinking her teeth into his dirt-smeared flesh.

He screamed and let go of her. She again tried to run towards Susanna, but another thief backhanded her across the face. The force of the blow spun her sideways and sent her careening into the table, which toppled beneath her weight.

Spencer laughed. "Bring her this way," he ordered, dragging Susanna down a hall and into the second open door – a bedroom.

"Get away from 'er!" Mary yelled, rushing forward and clawing at Spencer's arm. "Leave 'er alone!"

Spencer glared at her for a moment. "I believe this little missy is too much trouble for 'er own good," he declared.

Before either woman could react, he produced a small dagger and flicked it across Mary's throat. Susanna watched in muted horror as the flesh parted, spreading into a grotesque red smile below her maid's chin. The blood hesitated before it began to flow, rushing down to the floor in rivulets.

Mary's expression went from fury to shock, and then to fear. The girl went limp and slumped down onto the floor like a broken doll, legs splayed unnaturally beneath her. The front of her plain grey frock was now a dark crimson.

Susanna's eyes widened in horror. "Mary?" she whispered. "Mary!" She twisted in her captor's arms, limbs kicking and flailing like a hellcat. "*You bloody bastard! You bastard!*"

Spencer laughed uproariously and flung her roughly to the wooden floor. He dragged her by her hair into the bedroom. Before she could react, he was on top of her, holding her wrists above her head. She continued to fight him. A steady string of curses flowed from her mouth with such ease that even Spencer was momentarily taken aback.

***

Blair rammed his shoulder against the door. He heard the wood splinter and tried again. On his fourth pass, it gave with an uneasy groan. He stopped and looked around at the overturned table and splintered chairs.

His attention was drawn away from the destruction by the sound of a woman's desperate screams from down the hall. *Susanna*, he thought angrily. He started down the corridor at a run.

"*You bloody bastard! You bastard!*" the woman screamed. "*Rot in hell you damnable son of a whore!*"

Blair nearly tripped. That couldn't possibly be his fiancée shouting obscenities that would make even Ceallach blush. Could it?

"*I hope rats eat your eyes and the Devil pisses on your bones!*"

Good God, what had he gotten himself into?

"*Get off of me, you pig!*"

***

"Get off of me, you pig!" Susanna shrieked, trying to kick her legs. If she could just catch him between the thighs...Andrew had taught her that particular weakness when she'd accidentally hit him there with a stirrup once.

"Hush, *milady*," Spencer spat the word, breathing heavy against her ear. "Ye'll like me well enough in a moment. I'll make ye beg for me."

"Stop!" She continued to fight him and parted her legs slightly to better kick him.

Susanna realized her mistake too late, when he forced a knee between her thighs.

"There ye go, missy," he said with a grin. "Open up for me now."

"Please do not do this," she begged.

Spencer licked her face crudely and she turned her head to the side, squeezing her eyes shut. The man went to push up her skirts, and realized that he could not disrobe her without releasing his grip on her wrists.

"Hold her!" he grunted to one of his men.

One thief stepped forward obediently. "Why is it ye get to 'ave her first, anyway?" He took her wrists and stretched them out above her head.

Spencer glowered at him. "Because I like virgins. An' I intend to make 'er enjoy it. Can't ye see it in 'er eyes? She wants me."

Gathering her courage, Susanna raised her head and spat in his face. "I would rather bed a Scot than you, you louse!"

The noxious laughter of Spencer's men was cut short by a loud cough from the doorway.

"I'd be careful what ye wish for, my Lady," an unfamiliar voice commented. The accent was melodic, similar to that of the children she'd met the day before, only more pronounced. Susanna twisted her head and peered at the newcomer through the crook of Spencer's arm. A tall, broad-shouldered man stood just inside the door, leaning casually against the wall. His arms were crossed over his chest, and the muscles of his biceps rippled and bunched with raw, masculine power. His long, brown hair tumbled freely past his shoulders, four tiny braids grazing his cheeks. Cheeks which were whiskered by day-old stubble.

Susanna's gaze dropped lower to the perfectly sculpted muscles of his lower thighs and calves, completely bare below the plaid wrappings of his mantle.

"Go find yer own party," Spencer snarled over his shoulder.

The man seemed to contemplate the directive for a moment. Then he shook his head. "I canna let ye hurt the lass."

"I wish to enjoy her, Scot. Go yer way an' I'll forgive the interruption."

"How about this," her savior said, uncrossing his arms and taking a step forward. "Ye take yer hands off her now, and I'll merely break yer legs, as opposed to runnin' ye through with my sword."

Spencer gave the man an irritated look and reached into his boot to retrieve a dagger before he stood, turning to face the intruder. "Alright, Scot. I suppose now we fight."

"Yer damn right we do," he replied, drawing his sword.

Two of the thieves rushed him from opposite sides of the room. The Scot swung his sword in a wide, fluid arc, slicing both assailants across the ribs. The men dropped almost instantly, landing on the floor with a loud, collective 'thud'. Susanna took advantage of the chaos and scrambled to her knees, then crawled into the corner. She drew her knees to her chest and watched in mute fascination.

The Scot noticed her retreat and gave her an almost imperceptible nod. Then he looked back to Spencer. "Next."

The third minion approached alone, wielding a large broadsword. He swung and his opponent parried, and then riposted, driving his sword through the thief's gut with a grunt.

"Impressive, Scot," Spencer commented. "Ye must fancy her as much as I do. Don' think fer a second, my dear," he spoke over his shoulder to Susanna, "that he does not plan to enjoy ye 'imself."

Susanna's eyes widened.

"Ye had only two others, did ye no?" the Scot asked, unfazed. "The ones guarding the hall?"

Spencer cursed.

"Aye, I thought as much. That means it's yer turn."

Spencer ran at him, his dagger gripped tight in his left hand. The Scot growled and dropped his sword before charging, knocking Spencer off his feet. In a flash of movement, he had the dagger in his own hand, poised above Spencer's chest. He raised it up and stopped just short of plunging it into the man's heart. His eyes flicked to Susanna who was watching with a look of sheer terror, her knuckles pressed against her mouth.

"The lady has seen enough death fer today, but ye'll not hurt a woman ever again," he decided, adjusting his aim before driving the blade into Spencer's groin.

Spencer howled – a tortured, animalistic sound, and curled into a fetal position, cradling his ruined genitals.

Susanna saw her chance. She pushed to her feet and made a break for the door, hoping to run past both men and get to one of the horses outside. She'd ride back to Newcastle and get help. Perhaps she would find her two remaining guards there. But she would *not* stay here, only to be raped by the man who'd saved her.

Before she reached the hall, she caught sight of her dead handmaid, slumped grotesquely against the wall. Her legs buckled and the world went black.

Chapter Four

Blair was actually grateful that Susanna had fainted. He'd expected her to run from him, and he'd known she would have been frightened had he tried to stop her. Her loss of consciousness allowed him to carry her outside, away from the carnage that he'd caused inside the manor house.

Fantastic way to introduce yerself, he thought bitterly as he scooped her up into his arms and stepped carefully over the bodies littering the hall. *Saved her, aye, an' scared the hell out o' her, too.* Spencer still lay in a ball on the floor, moaning. Blair ignored him. The man might live, or he might die. Either was fine with the Scottish Lord, though he'd prefer the latter. It had only been Susanna's presence that had stopped him from slaughtering the thief like an animal.

Once outside, he took the opportunity to truly look at her for the first time. The tiny portrait in his bedchamber didn't do her justice. She was breathtaking, even with her dress torn and her face stained with tears. Her long eyelashes, glistening with teardrops, fanned over her cheeks, giving her a delicate, fragile quality. Her skin was pale and flawless. Two tiny freckles dotted the tip of her small, rounded nose, and her lips were slightly parted, full, soft, and begging to be kissed.

The longer he studied her, the more convinced he became that the English king was not so terrible after all.

She was so petite he held her easily. Her fingers – long, tapered, and smooth -- were curled into loose fists against his chest: a gesture that was innocent and sweet. Blair's skin burned where her body made contact with his, even through their clothing. The neckline of her gown was torn, exposing her long, slender neck. He silently cursed his body's reaction to her beauty, the way his groin tightened when his gaze dipped below the hollow of her throat and took in the high, firm swell of her breasts beneath the modest gown.

She'd been terrified of him as he'd fought off her kidnappers. He'd seen it in her eyes. The thought pained him. She believed him to be an untamed heathen and a fine job he'd done of convincing her otherwise. But he hadn't been thinking about that when he'd charged into the manor house to rescue her. He'd been thinking about keeping her safe, and that was all. No matter the cost. But now...

She stirred in his arms, letting out a soft moan. When she opened her eyes and stared up at him, he made a decision he knew he'd probably pay for later.

***

Warm. The first thing Susanna felt when she woke was warm. And, somehow, safe. Her head reeled with a heady, soothing scent – earthy and masculine – and she moaned, turning into the warmth and comfort. She opened her palm and encountered something hard, and at the same time, soft. If she didn't know better, she'd almost think she was...

Her eyes flew open. She was, indeed, in the arms of a man; a very large one, at that. Her head was resting against his broad, muscular chest, and she was cradled sideways in his arms. A smattering of dark curls peppered his chest, peeking out from beneath the bright pattern of his mantle. She gazed up into his face and her breath caught in her throat.

Good Lord in heaven, if he'd been handsome from afar, he was downright sinful up close. His skin was dark and tanned. An angular jaw line framed well-defined lips and a regal, aquiline nose. Blue eyes, liquid and intense, were set below thick, sculpted eyebrows; the same dark brown as his hair. He was looking at her with evident concern, and the crease between his brows deepened slightly. It added to, rather than detracted from, his beauty.

Oh, my, she thought before she could stop herself.

Only, judging from the way his lip curled into a charming half-smile, she hadn't so much *thought* it, as she'd *said it*.

"Are ye alright, lass?" he asked, supporting her weight entirely.

"Yes," she replied as she stiffened. "Yes, I am fine. You may release me now."

He arched one eyebrow but did as requested, setting her on her feet and taking a step backwards.

Susanna crumpled immediately. His arms shot out and caught her before she hit the ground.

"Apparently, ye are no fine, milady," he commented with a hint of amusement.

"I am glad you find the situation humorous," she responded curtly.

At that, his expression darkened. He looked genuinely offended. "Lass, I dinna find anything humorous about what happened to ye today. An' I, for one, am damned grateful I found ye when I did, whether ye be the same or no."

"I am of course grateful for your aid, sir." She looked at him again and her face softened. "Thank you," she said honestly.

"What's yer name, lass?"

"Susanna," she replied. "Yours?"

He paused. "James."

"Thank you, James, for saving my life," she repeated. She cocked her head and looked at him curiously. "You do not look like a James."

He seemed uncomfortable. "Well, ye should take that up with my mother, lass."

She gave him a sheepish smile. "Fair enough."

"What were ye doing out here by yerself, anyway?"

"I was not alone." It was her turn to be offended. "Half of my guard and my driver betrayed me. They gave me and..." she drew in a breath, "and my handmaid, Mary, to Spencer and his thieves." She would *not* cry and appear weak and foolish.

"I am sorry for yer loss," he said awkwardly.

She nodded and chewed her lower lip. "She tried to protect me. Everyone who tried to protect me died, except you."

"I am sorry," he repeated.

"I do not wish to inconvenience you any more than I already have, James, but..." Oh, this was hard. And possibly very foolish. She knew nothing about him, other than the fact that he'd saved her life, and had done nothing to harm her as she'd lain unconscious in his arms for God only knew how long. "If you are on your way to Newcastle, I would appreciate your company."

"Actually, my Lady, I was on my way to Perth," he replied. "When I came across yer caravan, it was headed north as well."

"I was, yes."

"Then it would make more sense if ye came with me north, lass."

"I..." she considered her options. Her escorts, those who had not betrayed her, were dead. If he took her back to Newcastle, what would she do? Send word to her father, wait for more guards, and then what? "I could not burden you in such a way."

"It seems no a burden, but logical, to me," James countered.

"Then it appears I shall be twice in your debt."

"Can ye walk, lass?"

Honestly, she didn't know. "Yes."

"My horse is there," he said, nodding at a large, chestnut stallion grazing several yards away. With a hand resting on the small of her back, he steered her towards the animal. It was the only horse that hadn't run off, apparently, as Susanna saw no sign of her own steed, nor those of Spencer and his men.

"Where is my horse?" she asked.

"I dinna ken. Ye'll have to ride with me, I'm afraid."

For some reason, she wasn't all that disturbed by the idea of spending more time in close proximity with him. But it wouldn't do to let *him* know that. "I suppose I have no choice," she said demurely.

***

Blair did his best to ignore the stirrings in his groin as he led Susanna to his horse. She really was petite, he noticed, the top of her head barely came to his shoulder.

It was going to be difficult to convince his fiancée that he wasn't a barbarian when he *felt* like one. Every time he looked at her he wanted to crush her against him and ravish her pretty little mouth, to feel her breasts pressed against his chest, to pull her hair free and run his fingers through it, to feel her long, red locks brushing his bare skin as she...

He shook his head. *Stop it*, he ordered himself silently.

He hadn't lied to her – not exactly. James was his middle name. He would tell her the truth soon, he vowed.

Blair helped her into the saddle and swung up easily behind her. It wasn't the most comfortable of places, with the back of the saddle digging into his groin. He grabbed the reins with one hand and, without thinking, wrapped his other arm around her waist. He felt her tense.

"I dinna want ye to fall off, lass," he said.

She relaxed again, leaning back against his chest. "May I take a few of my belongings?" she asked timidly.

"Aye, of course ye may." In fact, when he'd ridden past the caravan earlier, the mare had still been hooked to the small cart containing her luggage. He hoped that was still true, in which case he would simply tether the mare to his horse and she wouldn't be forced to leave any of her things behind at all.

As they crested the hill and the road came into view, Blair saw they were in luck. The luggage cart was in the grass several yards off the road, the mare attached to it grazing happily. He cringed at the two bodies that still littered the ground. Susanna's sharp intake of breath indicated that she'd noticed them, too.

"I know how Henry died," she said, "but who killed *him*? You?"

Blair shook his head. "He was dead when I came upon him."

Susanna seemed to accept this. She sighed as she took in the sight of her belongings scattered across the road.

"We'll pick them up, lass, an' pack everything onto the cart. Ye'll not have to leave any of yer things behind."

***

An hour later Susanna's dresses were repacked and all of her trunks were back on the cart. James had placed his saddle in with her belongings, and they sat bareback on his horse with the mare tethered and following behind.

Deciding there was little need for modesty or propriety, she rode with one leg on either side of the horse's considerable girth, her skirts tucked underneath. Her back rested against James' chest, and one of his arms circled her waist. She was surprised at how comfortable she felt with him given the violence she knew him to be capable of.

She glanced over her shoulder. He was facing forward, concentrating on the road ahead, his mouth pressed into a firm line. The wind stirred his hair and she again caught a hint of his scent.

Dear Lord, a man should not be this handsome.
"Do you know Lord Ruthven?" Susanna asked, mostly to distract herself.

He stiffened. "Aye, I know him."

"Is he... decent?" she ventured.

"I believe so. Why do ye ask?"

Susanna hesitated. She didn't want to tell him she was engaged to the man. She knew that the clans warred with each other constantly, clashing even more violently than England did with Scotland as a whole. If James was a member of an enemy clan, and he knew she was betrothed to Ruthven, he might use her to... she didn't want to think about it. "I have heard of him."

"What have ye heard?"

"That he is an assassin for King James," she admitted. "That he, well..."

"Rapes women, slaughters children, an' forces men to bow to his rule or else he steals their women as well? That he sleeps outside like a beast, an' eats his meat raw?" his mouth twitched.

"No...Well, maybe."

"Ah. Would ye like to know what we Scots tell our children? What yer king Henry does to little lads who dinna eat their suppers?"

"I... oh, damnation," she muttered.

James chuckled. "Ye have a very coarse tongue for a lady. Where did ye learn such language?"

"Chaucer. He wrote--"

"*Of deerne love he koude and of solas; and thereto he was sleigh and ful privee, and lyk a mayden meke for to see,*" he quoted.

"You have read *The Canterbury Tales*?" she asked incredulously, twisting in his arms to regard him.

"Aye. Between raiding an' pillaging I read a little," he deadpanned. At her sharp intake of breath, he flashed her a dazzling smile.

"You jest."

"Aye, lass, I do." He looked down at her and grinned again.

Susanna thought she might swoon. *Stop it! Stop it now!*

"For the record, milady, I havena ever raped a woman, nor have I harmed a child, nor stolen another man's wife. I have, on occasion, slept outside when the situation required it, but I prefer a bed an' a warm fire, an' I like my meat cooked thoroughly," he readjusted his grip on her waist and his fingers spread out across her stomach, in a gesture that was not quite a caress, but not entirely chaste, either.

She wasn't sure what to say to that, so she remained silent, doing her best to remain focused on the road ahead as opposed to the warm hand pressed against her middle.

"So," James said finally, "what else do ye like to read, lass?"

"My father brings me books from London," she replied. "I recently read *The Lover's Confession.*"

"John Gower," he identified. "They say he was a dear friend of Chaucer."

She was impressed. Again. "Yes, they do say that."

"So tell me, Lady Susanna, how it is that an intelligent, well-read woman such as yerself was on the road to Perth?" It was the first time he'd used her name, and she almost shivered at the way it rolled off his tongue, sounding like 'Soosena', with his accent.

"I am...meeting someone," she said lamely.

"Someone important?" he pressed.

"Someone I have never met."

"Ah, so he doesna expect ye, then?"

"No. I mean yes. I mean, I do not know, exactly. Why do you ask?"

"I was wondering if he'd miss ye, should I choose to carry ye off into the hills for myself," James answered.

She leaned back against his arm and craned her neck to gape at him. "You would not dare," she said in a horrified whisper, though in truth she was only partially horrified.

"No?" he winked at her.

"You are teasing me again!"

"Aye."

"Why?" her face flushed with embarrassment at having been fooled yet again.

"Because when I do, ye smile, an' it makes ye look verra pretty."

Her face reddened even more. "So do you," she mumbled, then froze, terrified at the admission. What was it about him that made her act like such a simpering fool?

"I look pretty when ye smile?"

It figured he wouldn't just ignore the slip. She started to stammer out a reply, but eventually snapped her mouth shut in frustration and turned around to face forward again. She felt his chest rub against her back as he bent down close to her ear, his breath warm against her cheek, stirring her errant curls.

"*As to my dome, in al Troyes citee,*" he recited, "*Nas noon so fair, for passing every wight so aungellyk was hir natyf beautee, that lyk a thing immortal seemed she...*"

Susanna smiled. "*Troilus and Criseyde,*" she identified. On impulse, she laid her head back against his shoulder and closed her eyes. After a moment he began to speak again, reciting the tale from memory, and before long, she was completely relaxed in his arms.

Chapter Five

They rode nonstop for the rest of the day. When they crossed the border into Scotland, he paused in his narration of *Troilus and Criseyde* long enough to point out subtle changes in the landscape. She opened her eyes and looked around.

"It is beautiful here," she commented.

It warmed his heart to hear her honest praise of the country he so loved.

She was less enthusiastic when Blair told her they would be spending the night outdoors.

"Is there no inn close by?" she asked.

"Nay, lass. Scotland is'na the wasteland ye've been told it is, but luxuries are fewer an' farther between than in yer native country. Ye'll be safer out here with me, anyway, then in some tavern."

"What if it rains?"

"Then ye'll get wet, lass," he replied jovially. "It willna kill ye."

"Can you promise I will not be attacked by some wild animal?"

Not if ye keep looking at me like that. "I swear it, milady," he declared theatrically, eliciting a giggle from her.

"Where shall we sleep, though?" she asked, as he pulled the horses off the road and led them into the woods.

"Anywhere we like."

Once they were far enough from the road to avoid notice, he brought the horses to a halt and dismounted, turning to help Susanna down. But she was no longer on the horse. "Lass?" he called.

"Yes?" she asked, peeking around the horse's flanks.

"How did ye get down here?" he asked, astonished that he hadn't heard her hit the ground.

"Well, I must have flown," she quipped, "since women are apparently incapable of knowing their way around a horse."

His lips twitched and he fought off a smile. "A lass who kin fly, but canna dismount a steed? Ye shall have to warn me next time ye take flight, as it is somethin' I would like to see."

She laughed. God, how he loved the sound of it. "So will we sleep here?" Susanna asked.

"Aye, it's a fine spot, don't ye think?" The sun was just slipping below the horizon, and the woods were bathed in a crimson glow. The birds were chattering happily amongst themselves.

"Aye," she mimicked, giving him a sideways smile.

He winked at her. "Verra good, lass. Now, I'll start a fire, an' then we shall see about yer supper."

"That," she replied happily, "you will leave to me."

***

Before James kindled a fire, Susanna had him retrieve one of her trunks from the cart. Once he'd returned to his task, she set about completing hers, and stubbornly refused to fill him in on what she was doing, even though he asked half a dozen times.

Mary had insisted the cook pack them an entire trunk of cured meats, sweetcakes, and breads. Though Susanna's handmaid was a lanky girl, she'd enjoyed eating, and had insisted that she have enough food to last a fortnight.

Mary. Susanna choked back a sob as an image of her handmaid hiding sweetcakes beneath her apron, and sneaking out of the kitchen, flashed before her eyes. Mary laughing as the cook chased after her with a wooden spoon until Susanna had stepped in and announced the food was for her. Mary timidly asking her charge if one day maybe – just maybe – Susanna might teach her to read.

Susanna pressed her hand over her mouth and fought away her tears. Concentrating on unpacking the food, she didn't hear James come to stand beside her.

"Ye canna feel guilty over things that werena yer fault, lass," he said gently. "Mary would fight an' die for ye all o'er again if she were able."

"It is not fair," she whispered.

"Nay. Few things in life are. But ye kin honor her memory. When ye are ready, I should like to hear about her."

Susanna nodded. "She liked to eat very much," she offered, gesturing to the food she had set aside for their meal.

James chuckled. "Are ye sure her parents werena Scots?"

She smiled at him. He was close by her side, but made no move to touch her. She wished he would. She'd liked having his arm wrapped around her all day, liked it more than she cared to admit.

They ate in silence, sitting before the small fire James had made. He'd pulled another of her trunks from the cart for her to sit on, but when she saw that he was content to sit on the ground, in the dirt, she did the same. Her gown was already torn, a little mud couldn't harm it any.

After they were both fed, he retrieved the blankets from his saddle roll and spread them over the ground as a makeshift bed for her. It didn't look to be the most comfortable thing but, then again, the flimsy straw mats she'd been sleeping on for the past week weren't much better. Though he offered to turn his back so that she could change, she elected to sleep in her ruined travel gown. Susanna loosed her hair – half of it having already come free of the pins anyway – and lay down.

***

She was asleep within moments. Blair stayed awake and watched her as she slumbered, memorizing every bit of her angelic face. Susanna was beautiful as she slept; her long lashes brushing her cheeks, her lips slightly parted, the faint rise and fall of her breasts. But she was even prettier when she was awake, in his opinion. When she laughed her cheeks dimpled, and her wide green eyes, so full of depth he thought he might get lost in them, sparkled. And when she was embarrassed or frustrated with him, she blushed in the sweetest way, making the freckles at the end of her nose darken just a tiny bit.

Throughout the day, it had become his goal to make her laugh or blush as often as possible. He was completely and utterly captivated by her. She was intelligent, for one. He hadn't let her know, but he'd been as surprised as she to learn that they'd read the same books and even spoke the same languages, with the exception of Susanna's knowledge of Greek, and Blair's of his native Gaelic.

She was good-natured, and he admired her sense of humor. Her impressive command of profane vocabulary continued to amaze him as well. There was something endearing about a woman not afraid to curse when the situation required it.

Blair lounged by the fire, his long, lean body stretched out, like a cat. He made sure to keep a good distance between them, though. Every time he was close to her he wanted to touch her, run his fingers through her hair, caress her cheek. He'd caught her looking at him several times with that expression he'd been known to evoke in women his entire life, one of unabashed appreciation. But he was determined not to force himself on her, nor to encourage her to do anything she would regret later.

A nearly inaudible whimper brought him out of his reverie. He looked over and saw that she was still asleep, and dreaming. From the look of her face, contorted into a cross between a frown and a sneer, and the fresh tears that sparkled on her eyelashes, the dream was not a pleasant one.

He surprised himself with how quickly he moved to kneel by her side. "Lass?" he asked softly.

She whimpered again and a single tear trickled from the corner of her eye.

"Susanna?" This time he reached out and touched her cheek.

She sat up with a gasp and a strangled cry. She moved to fight him, but then her gaze seemed to focus and recognize who he was. "James?"

"Ye were dreamin', lass," he said, and grazed her cheek with his knuckles again.

They were close – too close. He could feel her tiny exhalations on his skin. The warrior in him wanted to ravish her. The nobleman wanted much the same. She looked up at him, her big, green eyes full of emotion. Expectant. "Susanna," he breathed.

She continued to stare, as if waiting for him to make his choice.

If he tried to fight himself, he'd lose. She was a noble lady, not some country girl or serving maid or pretty courtier whose dignity meant nothing. She was going to be his wife.

His wife. She was already his. Dear Lord, he'd almost forgotten it. *She's mine*, he told himself. Only she didn't know that. But she would soon. He'd tell her tonight. Then it wouldn't matter what they did.

He kissed her.

***

Susanna had never in her life experienced anything more decadent. His lips on hers – his tongue exploring her mouth – rough and gentle at the same time. Soft and hard. She placed her palms against his chest and left them there, feeling his heartbeat, so strong. His arms came around her and pulled her tight against his body, so close she could feel every muscle.

Oh God, it was heaven. She moaned against his lips. He was running his hands up and down her back, sending little currents through her entire body, and when she moaned she felt his fingers tangle in the curls at the nape of her neck, angling her head to better plunder her mouth.

He was perfect. He was...

Not her fiancé.

Reality came slamming back with heartbreaking speed. *What am I doing?*

She pushed against his chest, pulling away from the kiss, and looked down. If she looked back into his eyes, and he moved to kiss her again, she didn't think she would have the willpower to stop him.

"Ye didna like it, lass?" he asked, his breathing a bit labored.

"I...oh hell," she muttered, extracting herself and turning away from his searing, hungry gaze. It wasn't enough, though; she could still feel his eyes on her, so she stood and tried to put some distance between them.

In an instant he was beside her. He put one arm around her waist, but quickly withdrew when he felt her tense. "Ye what?"

"I am engaged," she blurted. "I am on my way to Perthshire to be married." She closed her eyes and waited for him to rail at her. To tell her she was a wanton and a whore.

"Aye, I know," he answered.

"You *what*?"

"Ye are engaged to the Duke."

"You know who I am?" she asked, swiveling her head to regard him with moist eyes.

"The Lady Cavendish, I assume."

"How do you know?"

"I was sent to fetch ye," he confessed.

"Sent to fetch me?"

"Aye."

"You've known *the entire time*?"

"Aye."

"I...You...you *ass!*" she sputtered. Whirling on her heels, she stalked off into the woods.

***

"Wait, my Lady!" Blair called, running after her. He'd expected her to be relieved that he knew who she was. And he'd planned to use that revelation as a segue into telling her who *he* was. Instead and inexplicably, in his opinion, she was furious. "Susanna!"

He caught up with her easily and grabbed at her elbow. He wanted her against him again. Now. Even if she was angry. He ached for her and the absolute rightness that he felt when he touched her.

"Do not *touch me!*" she shrieked, jerking away from him as if burned.

"Susanna, please—"

"No!" She whirled to face him in pure fury. "This whole time! You have known *the whole damnable time*! What was this, some cruel joke? Or a test perhaps? A test of my virtue? Did my fiancé put you up to this?"

"Lass..." he started, hands held out, palms up in placation.

"Soil the foolish little English girl!" she fumed, her anger unabated. "Send her back to her father a ruined, wanton whore, send a message to the king! You bloody bastard!"

"Susanna," he tried again, reaching for her.

"I said *do not touch me*," she hissed, balling her fists. Then she did something that took him completely aback.

She slapped him. As hard as she could across the face. For such a tiny thing, she had a rather powerful forehand. His cheek stung and he rubbed at his jaw as he stared at her.

"Do ye feel better?" he asked sardonically.

"No I do *not*." She glared at him, chest heaving. Damn that dress she was wearing, he could quite clearly make out the swell of her breasts through the tear in the fabric. "So tell me, then, who are you? The stable boy? Or, perhaps, some man-for-hire? Just how low-brow have I made myself?"

Now that really was too far. Blair caught her by the arms and held her in place. He wanted to shake her until her teeth rattled.

"I dinna appreciate being slapped, lass," he growled, pulled her to him, and capturing her lips.

She tensed, as if ready to fight him again, and then she was kissing him back, hands clawing at his chest. He didn't have to draw her closer, she was already pressing her whole body against his. He could feel the small points of her nipples against his chest. Blair instantly hardened, every part of him rigid and alert – and hungry.

When he broke the kiss she reached up and grasped his face. "How dare you!" she whispered angrily, before yanking him back down to her again.

Thank God, he thought. He reached down with his left arm and scooped her up, not breaking their kiss. Her arms immediately wound around his neck and her hands tangled in his hair. She was growing bolder, trying to mimic his movements, making tentative forays into his mouth with her tongue. He traced the line of her teeth, stroked her tongue with his, and then withdrew, encouraging her to copy the gesture.

All traces of Susanna's anger seemed to have disappeared, replaced by an innocence and a passion that had him half out of his mind. He walked back to her blankets and lowered himself to his knees, to set her on the ground, before easing her onto her back. He stretched out beside her.

"James," she whispered. In the firelight, he could just barely make out that same, wide-eyed stare that had made him kiss her in the first place.

Blair, he wanted to say. *Call me Blair.*

***

"Stop," she whispered. "James, please. You have to stop."

"Why?" he continued, undeterred. He ran his lips along her neck. One hand trailed up her side, just grazing her breast. Then his hands were at her back, undoing her gown with practiced precision.

Oh, yes...

No! "You have to."

"Why?" he asked again. His tongue circled the shell of her ear before he took the lobe between his teeth, making her whimper.

"I am engaged," she managed to gasp.

"Aye, we've covered that."

"I am a virgin."

"I know." He rose up and looked at her tenderly, cupping her cheek with one hand. "And I willna take that from ye, but I do plan to kiss ye breathless."

"What if I said I did not want you to kiss me?" She was trembling. Damn her body for betraying her, and damn him for making her feel this way.

"Then I would say ye were lyin'."

He pulled her gown from her, tossing it aside, and then slipped her arms through the sleeves of her shift, pushing away the fabric until her upper body was bare. Her breasts were firm and proud, her nipples dark-rose.

"Gorgeous," he said reverently, skimming his palm under one breast to test its weight in his hand. His thumb brushed over her nipple, which immediately hardened.

She shivered. James dipped his head and took the tiny peak into his mouth. As he suckled her, rolling the nub against the roof of his mouth, Susanna let her eyes drift closed. One of his hands traced patterns across her stomach, pausing occasionally to give her other breast a gentle squeeze. She moaned and squirmed beneath him and when he shifted his attention to her right breast, she allowed her legs to part slightly, enough that if he wanted to...

He stopped himself each time his fingers drifted below her navel, and several times she thought she heard him groan.

Just when she was certain he would try to bed her – a request she was in no state to refuse – he pulled away. He kissed her lips, then her cheeks, her eyelids and, finally, her forehead, before gathering her into his arms. "Get some sleep now, lass, before I lose control of myself."

"You said you only wanted to kiss me," she murmured, nuzzling his chest.

"And so I did," he replied, resting his chin against her hair. "If ye misunderstood where, that is'na my problem."

Chapter Six

Susanna had thought, as she'd drifted to sleep the night before, that she would be ashamed when she woke in the morning. But as her eyes fluttered open and she felt James' arms around her, all she could feel was content. She shifted to look at him. He was still asleep, but his embrace tightened reflexively, as if he thought she might try to run from him.

She settled against his chest, dropping her head back to watch him. She'd tried, throughout the day, to steal glances at him, to study him when he wasn't paying attention, but he'd seemed to always know when she was staring at him, and had caught her more than once. Now, he was sleeping, and she could look her fill without being embarrassed. And if he woke up, well...she was lying half-naked in his arms, she figured she'd earned a lengthy peek.

Susanna adored his face. She ran one finger down the ridge of his perfectly sculpted nose, over the tiny cleft above his upper lip, and then down along his chin. She traced his jaw line and, on impulse, craned her neck to kiss his chin, her lips following the path her fingers had taken. He had several days worth of stubble and she liked the way it felt, rough.

Yes, this was definitely a much better way to explore, she decided, as she kissed along his neck, and then across his collarbone.

His entire chest was tanned and dark, his nipples only slightly darker. She circled one tiny nub with her index finger, enjoying the feel of the pebbled flesh. She pressed her lips to it, paused, and then traced it with her tongue.

Susanna heard a sharp intake of breath and jerked her head up to see James, most definitely awake, watching her with a hooded gaze.

"Good morn," she said.

He flashed her a smile. "Good morn to ye, lass."

"How long have you been awake?"

"A while." His grin widened.

"And you did not tell me? I would like to have known that small fact," she said in feigned annoyance.

"Why, is there something ye need?"

"I'd like..." she glanced up at him shyly. *Oh, why not...* "I should like you to kiss me some more."

"Are you sure ye dinna wish to continue yer explorations? I kin pretend to be asleep again, if ye like."

"Perhaps later. It is not as fun when you are awake."

"Oh, I disagree, lass. I think it is far more enjoyable when I am."

Susanna felt something very hard pressing against her stomach. She was relatively naïve, but she'd had enough late night conversations with Mary to have a pretty good idea of what the *something* was.

He took notice of her blush and in one, fluid motion rolled over so that she lay beneath him. She gasped at the sensation of a man's weight on top of her for the first time.

James pulled back. "Have I hurt ye?"

"No."

"Would ye still like for me to kiss ye, then?"

"Oh, yes," she sighed, her breasts quivering against his chest. "Please."

He shocked her utterly when, after a quick peck on the lips, he slid down her body and settled between her thighs.

***

He was going to get himself into major trouble when he finally revealed his identity. But right now, he honestly didn't give a damn. He didn't know what it was about her that made him not care that they were in the middle of the woods, less than a hundred paces from the road. He wanted to make her scream. Her shift was still pooled around her waist, and he pushed the fabric up her body so that it bunched around her middle, leaving bare her luscious breasts and pale, slender legs.

"James?" her voice was tinged with apprehension. "What are you doing?"

"Kissin' ye, lass."

"Down *there*?" She tensed as he ran his lips along her inner thigh.

"Aye. Here."

"But I'm a—"

"Ye still will be, I promise." Blair pulled back to look at her – the soft, pink folds of her sex, barely visible beneath the tuft of auburn curls. Was any part of her not perfect?

He ran his tongue along the length of her, a slow, steady sampling, and was pleased to discover her already slightly moist. *God,* he was going to explode just from the taste of her. Which, considering that he had no intentions of taking her virginity until she knew who he was, would probably be just fine.

"Oh, good Lord," she moaned.

I agree. He sampled her again, pausing this time to gently ease his tongue inside her. His cock twitched. Blair licked at her entrance, lazy strokes, imitating the act another part of his anatomy was screaming at him to complete.

Susanna's hands covered his, resting on her spread thighs, and he laced their fingers together, relishing the absolute intimacy of the moment. He directed his attention to the sensitive bundle of nerves at her apex, coaxing the tiny bud from beneath its sheath.

She shrieked when he made contact with her clit, attempting to pull away from him before thrusting her hips forward against his face. It wasn't long before she was quivering and mewling loudly, back arched, holding his hands in a vice-like grip. He gave her fingers a reassuring squeeze and quickened his strokes, swirling his tongue around the sliver of flesh. Then he closed his lips around her and sucked.

Blair was actually grateful that they were hidden away in the woods, because when she came she screamed loud enough to raise the dead. He had *never* had a woman react with such absolute abandon to his touch.

He continued to guide her through her climax, and when her tremors began to subside, he plunged his tongue into her silky heat, sending her into a second euphoric tailspin.

When she finally went limp beneath him, he crawled up her body, pausing occasionally to plant gentle kisses along her sweat-soaked skin.

"James?" she interrupted his ministrations.

"Aye, lass?"

"How do I..." she trailed off and looked away, blushing furiously.

"How do ye what?" He honestly wasn't trying to tease her this time. He didn't know what she wanted.

"I want to..." she fell silent again, and he could tell from her expression that she was thinking desperately, trying to put the request into words. Finally, she slipped her hand between their bodies and brushed it over his groin.

His whole body convulsed at the unexpected contact. "Ye do no have to do that, Susanna," he said, even as he pushed forward to meet her palm again.

"I know. I want to. But..." she looked at him with those wide, green eyes and bit her lip. "I do not know how. Will you show me?"

If I last more than an instant... He rose into a kneeling position and unwound his mantle, tossing it aside, before lying on his back. He made to reach for her, but she was already at his side, her hand going to his rigid length.

Susanna closed her fingers around him, and he sucked his breath between his teeth. He thrust up into her palm, his control waning.

"Show me," she said again, fisting him tentatively.

He couldn't speak. He closed a hand over hers and guided her movements, up and down his cock. If she was disturbed by his nakedness, she didn't show it. She merely peered at him with a combination of eagerness and fascination. With his free hand, he threaded his fingers through her hair, pulling her down to capture her lips.

Susanna kissed him hungrily, then pulled away and bent her head over his prick, taking just the tip of him into her mouth. *She is an angel*, he thought as he felt his orgasm build with frightening speed. *My angel.*

He barely managed to yank her head away before he climaxed. He didn't want to startle her when it happened, and he'd been too caught up to explain. He came with a loud, triumphant roar.

Susanna's eyes went wide as she watched his seed coat his belly.

"Dear lord," she whispered. "Does it *always* do that?"

***

For the second time that day Susanna knew, deep within the recesses of her subconscious, that she should feel guilty about her actions. But the wild, rebellious part of her – the part that had made her kiss the stable hand, the part that allowed curses to slip past her lips with easy familiarity – was overjoyed at her rather thorough revolt against the societal expectations of her noble status.

"The river is'na far, lass," James commented. He was lying on his back with one arm propped behind his head, a lazy grin sneaking across his features.

"You are filthy," she agreed, eyeing his torso. She lay on her side next to him.

His free hand traced her breasts, tweaking her nipples, and then slipped between her legs to caress the silky skin of her inner thighs. "I would guess ye've never seen a man receive pleasure before."

"Certainly not." Her gaze drifted lower to where his cock lay against his stomach, soft and flaccid after his release. She blushed and turned her head.

"Ye kin look all ye like, lass," he offered, amused.

Her face grew redder. She took notice of his hand still between her thighs, stroking lightly, patiently. His middle finger brushed the folds of her sex and she shivered. Curiosity got the better of her and she found her eyes drifting back down along the planes of his torso, following the 'v' of muscles that led to his groin.

He began to harden again beneath her studious inspection. She looked up at his face and he smiled, lifting his eyebrows in suggestive invitation. She trailed her index finger through his wiry curls, then traced his cock, from the wide base up to the flared head. The skin was silky and smooth, and when she swept along his length again she added a second finger, then a third. He twitched against her, so she opened her palm and curled a fist around him.

"Susanna," he murmured, sliding one finger inside her.

She gasped and squeezed his prick reflexively at the unexpected invasion. Fluid rushed from her womb to coat his hand and she rotated her hips to receive more of the decadent sensation.

James rolled her beneath him, the sticky mess on his torso now coating her stomach and breasts, too. He continued to tease her, pushing a second finger into her tight heat. His cock, wrapped firmly within the sheath of her fingers, was close enough that, with one slight shift, he would be inside of her.

His fingers mimicked the movements of her hand. When she drew her fist down the length of his shaft, he thrust, and when she skimmed her palm up to his tip, he withdrew.

She keened loudly when he swiveled his hand, settling the pad of his thumb over her clit.

"Imagine," he whispered hotly against her ear, "me inside of ye like this."

"Yes," she moaned, rocking against his hand. "Please."

"Ye arena ready for that, sweetheart," he murmured. "Just imagine it for now."

But Susanna *was* ready; all she could think of was his cock buried within her, and she was about to tell him exactly that when he kissed her, his tongue moving in perfect harmony with their hands.

Her climax was even more explosive than the last had been. She screamed into his mouth and shook uncontrollably, her fist squeezing his cock in inadvertent simulation. Moments later, James joined her, and this time he did not pull away, but rather, held her close as his release bathed her breasts, just as hers covered his palm.

"I really must insist on a bath now, lass," he commented, when their breathing had returned to normal and her tremors had subsided.

"I will not protest."

She allowed him to pull her into a sitting position. Then he stood and bent over, scooping her up in his arms. He placed a kiss on her forehead. "Ye are the most extraordinary woman I have ever met, Susanna."

"I wager you say that to all the women you seduce," she replied sleepily, resting her head against his shoulder.

"Ye are the first. I am no virgin, but I have never felt with any other lass what I feel with you."

***

As a child, Susanna had dreamed of what it would be like to marry for love, but had never allowed herself more than the passing fantasy. Now, she felt like an adolescent with the way her heart desperately grasped at the flicker of hope that James would whisk her away with him, and they could live together, happy, just the two of them. No Dukes, or Kings, to dictate the course of her life. In her daydream there was only James, and she imagined herself the happiest she'd ever been.

James seemed equally reluctant to abandon the connection they'd formed. After their lovemaking -- which he still insisted upon referring to as 'kissing' -- and their bath, he dressed her, choosing a modest traveling gown of dark green fabric from her trunk. He even brushed her hair. At his request, she left it down, curling past her shoulders in an auburn sheen. He took his time packing up their small, impromptu camp.

"You are a Ruthven," Susanna said, watching him from her perch on a fallen log.

"I am."

"So will I..." she looked away, embarrassed by her own vulnerability, "Will I see you again after we reach Perthshire?"

"Ye will."

"Are you certain?" She was hopeful, even though she knew it would make her obligations more painful – to see him and have to deny what they'd shared.

"I am verra certain, lass. Ye will see me quite often, I promise ye."

"Do you think he will know?"

"Will who know what?" He was strapping the last pack to his horse's flanks.

"The Duke. Will he knows that we... I mean that you, and I..."

James turned and gave her an amused smile, eyes twinkling. "Aye, he'll know."

Her propriety kicked in. *Cavende tutum*, her father's voice whispered to her. Dear Lord, what would he say if he knew she'd nearly surrendered her purity to one of her fiancé's own men? Even Mary would have throttled her for this one. If James had told her no one would know, she would have grasped at the excuse to continue the affair, reasoning that she was allowed this one brief indulgence. Instead, he'd confirmed her fears of discovery. She had to distance herself from him, no matter how painful it was. She couldn't be with him, she was promised to his Laird. The sooner they both accepted it, they easier it would be.

And, in truth, it was probably for the best. All Susanna knew of love was what she'd read in her books, and they all ended in tragedy. Criseyde had betrayed Troilus. At least a stone heart could not be broken. "Perhaps I should ride the mare today," she suggested.

"Why?"

"It would be for the best, I believe, to not be so near you."

"My lady, I thought ye liked being near me," he replied suggestively.

"I apologize for giving you an unfair perception of my opinion of our situation," she responded in a flat, unfeeling tone.

All the mirth disappeared from his expression. He dropped the leather strap he'd been holding and strode over to her, before crouching and taking her chin in one hand. "What troubles ye, Susanna?"

"Nothing. Please ready the horse."

"Did yer mother never tell ye that ye lie horribly?" he teased, grazing her cheek with his knuckles.

Susanna looked away and shut her eyes. "My mother is dead."

He sighed. "Susanna, I'm sorry. I didna know."

"How could you have?" She turned back to him and set her mouth into a firm line, willing her eyes to go cold. "Are we far from Perth? The sooner we arrive, I think, the better."

"Have I offended ye in some manner, lass?"

"No." Oh God, if she looked at him anymore she would lose her resolve. The concern on his face made her chest ache.

"Well, I willna allow ye to ride the mare," he declared, standing and extending his hand.

"Why not?"

"Because."

"Because?" She stood, but did not accept his proffered hand. Susanna strode to the horse and attempted to mount the animal herself. After her third try, she turned and glared at him, hands on her hips. "If I am to ride with you, I require your help. I cannot get on this damn thing myself."

He helped her onto the horse without a word, then swung up behind her, one hand going around her waist while the other took hold of the reigns. As if on impulse, he paused and cupped her breast before spurring the horse forward.

Susanna fought off a sigh, and the urge to lean back against him. "I would ask that you not touch me like that again," she said instead.

"Why the hell no?" She could tell from his tone that he was confused and hurt.

"The shock of my abduction and the death of my friend have caused me to behave recklessly," she said, squeezing her eyes shut against the threatening onslaught of tears. *Because I love you*, she wanted to say. *God help me, I think I love you.*

"How so?"

"I acted improperly in my over-familiarity with you."

"I dinna object, lass."

"But I am sure my future husband would. I doubt he would appreciate my using one of his men in any way, least of all for my own empty, carnal gratification."

"Empty?" he asked tersely. She felt his arm go rigid.

"Regrettably so." Susanna kept her gaze focused on the road.

"Lady Cavendish," James said, and his arm fell away completely. "It is I who am regretful."

Chapter Seven

Ye are acting like a damn woman, Blair told himself angrily.   And God help him, he was. Susanna's harsh statements had hurt. 'Empty, carnal gratification', was that really all she thought of the time they'd spent together? It hadn't been empty for him. For the first time in his life, he'd made love to a woman.   He hadn't fucked her, or simply gotten himself off. Susanna warmed his heart.

He didn't think of their marriage as an obligation any longer. He hadn't thought that since the moment he'd seen her. No, they'd been united by God, not by two power-hungry kings.   She had to feel it. Something this powerful, this tangible, could not be his imagination -- his emotion -- alone. A man who had always relied upon brute, warrior strength, he could not have become such a love-struck fool all on his own.

Love-struck.   That was exactly what he was. Susanna was beautiful, there was no question of that – she had an angelic prettiness that even his brother would be hard pressed to find flaw in. But it wasn't her beauty that made him ache for her like a young lad chasing a village girl around the courtyard, it was *her*. Never one to do things only half-way, Blair had welcomed the possibility of a happy marriage between them, had embraced the idea of loving her, and she him. And now... he'd cut his right arm off if it would make her talk to him again.

They rode in silence.

The landscape changed, grew wilder, more rugged, as they approached the borders of his land. The gentle swells of hills were now tree-covered mountains – not the rocky, dizzying crags of the deep Highlands, but soft, lush monuments to his country's impressive beauty. They passed a loch, surrounded by fields of heather on one side, and large, deciduous trees on the other. Blair wanted to speak, to point out important landmarks and give her their names. He also wanted to lay her down amongst the flowers and make her beg for him again. But he would not be the first to break the silence. He was too conflicted to attempt conversation anyway.

Susanna's back was ramrod straight. She kept her face forward, and he could not make out her expression without being obvious about looking at her, which he pointedly refused to do. All of the barriers he'd knocked down between them had returned tenfold. He missed her laugh, her smile, the way she leaned against him with her eyes nearly closed, completely relaxed and trusting in his arms.

They crossed into his territory mid-afternoon. He didn't bother to announce their arrival; he didn't think she'd care. When the sun began to set, he led their small caravan off the road into the woods. They traveled a short while longer, until he found the spot he wanted – the small loch where, as a child, he'd learned to swim with his brother.

"We camp here tonight," he said, halting the horse and swinging down. He strode over to secure the mare, but didn't bother to offer her help dismount.

"How much farther to Perth?" she asked, clambering down.

"Half a day. We crossed onto Ruthven land some time ago."

"And we cannot keep going? Ride at night?"

"Nay." The truth was they were a hell of a lot closer to his castle than half a day's ride. His family seat was just beyond the small stretch of wood, across the valley at the base of the mountains. In fact, there was a tiny farm less than five hundred paces from where they'd stopped, which was exactly why he couldn't let them go any farther tonight.

There were Ruthvens living everywhere between here and the castle, and all of them knew their laird. Blair couldn't risk one of them addressing him in front of Susanna before he'd had a chance to tell her who he was.

After his initial flash of indignation at her rejection, some of his confidence had returned and he'd begun plotting. He knew she was attracted to him, knew she wanted him. It made sense that her proper, English upbringing would conflict with her desire, that she'd feel guilty about the things they'd done together, particularly when she didn't realize he was her fiancé. If he could show her how right they were together, that she belonged to him...then he could tell her his identity. All he needed was a way to break through her defenses. He'd done it once. He could do it again.

***

The day had been excruciating for Susanna. At least a dozen times she'd nearly crumbled. She wanted to turn around and fling herself at him, to smother him in kisses and beg his forgiveness for the harsh words she hadn't meant. She wanted to lay bare her heart and let him do with it what he would.

If he didn't feel the same way about her as she did about him, then tomorrow she would start her new life with the Duke and be no more miserable than if she'd held her tongue. But if he did care about her, perhaps they could find a way...

"James?" She kept her back to him, pretended to be studying something fascinating about the horse's flank. He was piling branches to make a small fire, she could hear the rustling as he stacked them methodically in the small clearing.

"Aye?" The rustling ceased.

"Do you..." she trailed off, took a deep breath. *Do you love me as I love you*? She couldn't say it. Lord help her, she couldn't say it.

"Do I what, lass?"

"Nothing."

"Susanna," he said, and his voice was soft near her ear.

She whirled around, startled that she hadn't heard him approach her. They were standing so close that her breasts touched his chest each time she inhaled. "Nothing," she mumbled again.

"Why do ye lie to yerself, and to me, lass?" he asked. His expression was stern, but his eyes were soft, almost pleading.

"I am not lying," she replied, looking away.

"Ye are," strong fingers gripped her chin and turned her to look at him once more. "Ye want me, milady. I see it in yer eyes, every time I lose myself in them."

"I do not," she insisted stubbornly.

"Then look me in the face and tell me so."

She met his gaze. "I do not want you," Susanna whispered, but she faltered as she said it, her eyes flicking away and back again, and he saw it.

He stroked her lower lip with his thumb. "I think ye do, luaidhe."

She shivered. "What does that mean...luaidhe?" She was trying desperately to focus on something, anything, other than the growing heat between her legs and his enticing touch.

"It means 'beloved' in Gaelic," he supplied. He brought his other hand up to stroke her cheek. "I shall teach ye to speak it."

"I'd like that." Her eyes fluttered closed.

"May I kiss ye, Susanna?" She could feel his breath on her lips, knew that he had bent his head in anticipation of her answer.

She placed her palms on his chest and melted against him, pressing her lips to his.

He had her gown off and had laid her down before she could protest, covering her with his strong, warm body, his arms braced on either side of her. She wrapped herself around him, spreading her legs and hooking her ankles at the small of his back.

"God, Susanna," he groaned, grinding against her. The friction of his cock through her thin shift sent sparks to her clit. She grew wet, opening for him like a flower.

Her hips rose up to meet his, her movements inexperienced and unrefined, but full of need.

She struggled to pull her shift up over her head but he caught her hands, lifting them above her head instead. "If ye take that off, I willna be able to stop myself," he grunted. "I'll be inside ye."

"It is what I want, you were right," she begged, not caring how shameless she sounded. "Take me. I want it to be you."

"Soon, luaidhe," he murmured, taking one hand off her wrists to smooth her hair back from her forehead. "I promise."

But there couldn't be a soon, and Susanna knew it. Tomorrow they would reach the castle. Tomorrow she would be presented to the Duke, and she would be forced to forget everything she'd ever felt for James in order to be a loyal wife. And that knowledge hurt – it hurt a lot.

She didn't bother to fight back her tears this time. She sobbed helplessly beneath him, even as she climbed towards orgasm, and when she cried out his name, it was both in pleasure, and in pain.

***

Morning found them together, limbs entwined, Susanna's head tucked beneath his chin. She was awake and crying softly, he could feel her tremble every now and again.

"Have ye heard the tale of the Lothian Farmer's wife, lass?" he asked, absently stroking her hair.

"The what?" she sniffed. "No."

"There was a farmer's wife many years ago who was carried off by the fairies. One year, she began to reappear on Sunday, amidst her bairnes, combin' their hair. On one of these occasions her husband caught her, an' demanded to know why she'd left him in such a manner. An' so she told him of her abduction, an' instructed him as to how he might win her back. She told him he must exert all his courage, for her eternal happiness rested upon his success."

Susanna sniffed again. "Go on."

"Now, the farmer loved his wife verra much, an' so he set out on Hallowe'en to wait for the fairies in a plot o' furze. First he 'eard the ringin' of the fairy bridles as their horses approached. When he 'eard the unearthly sound of the cavalcade. His heart failed him, an' he allowed the procession of ghosts to pass without interruption. When the last fairy had ridden past, the entire lot 'o 'em vanished amidst laughter an' celebration, an' among the voices he clearly heard his beloved wife, cryin' that he had now lost her forever."

"Well, that is not a very happy tale. Though I suppose that is fitting, given the circumstances."

"I shall no lose ye, milady," he whispered against her hair. "My courage shall no fail me, though I confess I need it greatly now."

"For what?" her sobs had quieted some.

"We need to talk."

"No, we do not," she replied, extracting herself from his embrace. She sat up and ran her fingers through her hair before wiping her cheek with the back of her palm.

"There is something ye must know, lass."

"Please help me dress, James," she said with a sniff, reaching for her gown and then slipping into it.

He stood and went to her, deftly lacing the back of the garment. When she was secured into it he tried to turn her to face him. "Susanna."

"Every time you want to talk I become a simpering fool and end up doing something I regret. Please, just take me to the castle." She refused to turn around and look at him.

"No before we've spoken."

"About what? The fact that I am going to be the Duchess?"

"Exactly. I willna take ye there until ye listen to me."

"Then I will walk there myself!" Susanna exclaimed. She whirled around and began walking through the woods.

"Lass, come back. This is nonsense."

She ignored him.

With a growl, Blair started off after her. She broke into a run. "Susanna!" he bellowed, lengthening his stride. He reached her just as she broke through the clearing and came face to face with a young peasant woman.

He wasn't sure who looked more startled – Susanna, or the woman. No more than twenty, the girl was busy gathering kindling. She dropped the branch she was holding and straightened, casting a glance over her shoulder at the small, thatched hovel several paces away.

"Mama!" a young voice called from inside the house. "Mama!"

Not bloody good, he thought, as he watched the youngster come barreling out the door. The lad saw him and shrieked, recognizing him instantly. Blair swore beneath his breath.

***

"He's back!" the child cried happily. "Mama, it's the Laird!"

The woman dropped into a curtsy. "Yer Grace. Ye are more than welcome to whatever my humble home has to offer."

Susanna gaped at him. "Your Grace?" she asked in a muted whisper. *No. No, not possible. He would have told me. He would have...*

He ignored her. "I thank ye for the offer, Ruadh, but the Lady is anxious to see her new home."

It was Ruadh's turn to appear surprised. "Ye're the new Duchess, then?" she asked, looking Susanna over. "Ye are more beautiful that we'd even dared to hope."

"Is that so?" Susanna asked dazedly.

James inclined his head at Ruadh and grasped Susanna's elbow. "She is verra tired from the journey. But perhaps once she is settled ye'd like to help her with her weddin' gown, Ruadh? Ye are by far the best seamstress in the clan."

The young woman blushed. "Oh, yer Grace, I couldna accept such an honor!"

"Ye can, an' ye will. I'll have Ceallach send for ye an' the wee one," James said to her.

"Do ye need a horse, yer Grace?" Ruadh asked. "My husband is just behind the house, we'd be happy to lend ye our steed."

"Nay, we have our own," he said smoothly. "The Lady wished to walk for a bit to stretch her legs, is all."

"Thank you for your kindness, Miss," Susanna interjected, recovering some of her wits. "But I believe we must be going."

"Aye, of course," Ruadh replied. "I shall wait for ye to summon me, yer Grace. Milady." She curtsied again before scooping up her son and heading into the house.

The conversation barely registered as she allowed James to turn her around and steer her back towards the horses. *Your Grace... she called him 'your Grace'. Oh God, he can't possibly be.*

"Let me go right now," she demanded.

"No."

She attempted to twist out of his grasp. He picked her up and tossed her over his shoulder. "That was verra imprudent of ye, Susanna."

Her shock was rapidly transitioning into anger. "Damn you, let me down!"

"No until we've had a civilized discussion." He carried her without effort, one of his large hands resting casually on her rear.

"I cannot have a civilized discussion with anyone who has me slung over his shoulder like a felled stag!"

He snorted and gave her ass a smack in response. When he reached their camp he set her down on her feet and crossed his arms over his chest. She immediately took several steps backward, putting as much distance between them as she thought he would allow before grabbing her again.

"Your name is not James," Susanna stated.

"It is, actually, Blair James Ruthven," he clarified.

"Duke of Perthshire."

"Aye."

"My fiancé," she whispered.

"This is'na how I wanted ye to find out, Susanna."

"Well it must have been, *your Grace*," she spat, "because in the two days we have spent alone together you have never once mentioned it."

"I wanted to tell ye, lass, but I dinna ken how."

"I see. Perhaps I am daft, I cannot help but think 'I am your future husband' would have been sufficient."

"I wanted..." he sighed and raked a hand through his hair. "Susanna, I wanted ye to see some other side of me before ye knew who I was, something beyond my ability with a sword. If I'd told ye when we first met who I was, ye'd a been scared of me. I wanted ye to get to know me."

"How the bloody hell could I get to know you if I thought you were someone else?" she demanded, fists clenched at her sides.

"Who did ye think I was?"

"Obviously not my fiancé!"

"I was going to tell ye, Susanna, I swear it. Before we reached the castle. I was," he said, and sighed again.

"But how about when you kissed me the first time?"

"I was going to—"

"Or when you told me you knew *my* identity?"

"I tried, ye were angry with me."

"Or when you stripped me naked and—"

"Damn ye, woman!" he roared, cutting her short.

"No. No, damn *you*. You have enjoyed my body enough, but apparently do not respect my intelligence at all!" She knew as soon as she'd said it that she'd gone too far. As usual.

"Of course I respect ye," he retorted. "If I dinna, I would have taken yer virginity when ye begged me to. Either the first, or the second time."

If she'd been within striking distance, she would have slapped him. "I see very little difference between the actual act of consummation and what we shared in the dirt, like animals, I might add. You are a cruel, miserable bastard. I curse the day the King signed our marriage contract."

His face contorted, lips twisting into an angry sneer. Then, just as quickly, his expression went blank again.

"I nearly trusted you with my virtue," she seethed.

"And ye still will, lass," he replied flatly, "as I am to be yer husband, an' will no be denied what is rightfully mine."

"I will honor you as a wife honors a husband, your Grace, but I have already been made twice the fool by you. I will not trust you with my heart so that it may happen yet again."

Chapter Eight

"Get on the horse, Susanna."

"No," she lifted her chin and glared at him. "I would prefer to ride in the cart with the rest of your belongings and *things that are rightfully yours*."

Blast if she hasn't become the most infuriating woman I've ever known. He crossed his arms and met her stubborn gaze with one of his own. "Get on the horse, lass, or I shall put ye there myself, tied hand to foot o'er my lap."

"I would not sit willingly on the same continent with you, your Grace, let alone on the same horse."

"As milady wishes," he replied with a shrug. Before she could turn and flee, he picked her up and flung her onto the horse's back, then swung up behind her. With one arm around her waist, he pulled her into his lap.

"Let me down you oaf!" she shrieked, pounding against his thigh.

"I dinna think so, luaidhe. Now settle down before ye spook the horses."

"You cannot expect me to ride to my new home like this!" She glared up at him from beneath a mass of disheveled curls, green eyes flashing. Her curved bottom was thrust up enticingly at him, so he gave her a light smack.

To his surprise, she let out a tiny sigh. He felt her nipples tighten into hard points against his thigh and she raised herself, ever so slightly, into his cupped palm.

Even through his anger and frustration, Blair's cock swelled and he had a sudden urge to slip his hand beneath her gown. "Actually, lass, I expected ye to ride in my arms like a lady, but ye refused to do so. If ye promise to behave, I might be persuaded to reconsider."

Her eyes narrowed. "Fine."

"Fine what?" He fought off a smile.

"Fine, I will behave."

He raised an eyebrow at her.

"I promise," she added dourly.

"There. That wasna so bad, was it?" he asked, knowing he was making her more furious with him. He lifted her up and sat her down in front of him, then slipped an arm around her waist and held it there.

"I can behave myself without you groping me, thank you very much," she huffed, trying to push his arm away.

Blair chuckled and pulled her tight against him, the roundness of her rear pressing into his erection.

"You are a brute!" she hissed, attempting to wiggle away from him. Her struggling did nothing more than create a rather delicious friction against his groin.

"Lass," he grunted, trying to hold her still, "ye are not having the effect ye desire with yer squirming."

She stilled immediately and swore under her breath.

"Has anyone ever told ye that ye are beautiful when yer angry, luaidhe?" he murmured against her cheek. "I am glad ye are so feisty."

"Yes, I can tell," she commented dryly. "I hope it withers and falls off."

"But if that happened, our marriage would be a boring one indeed."

"You are a brute," she said again.

"Ye are the one who brought up the topic of my manhood, lass."

"I did not!"

"No? I believe ye—"

"Stop it. I am ending this foolish conversation. I refuse to be baited by you!"

Blair chuckled again but fell silent, the steady rustling of the horses' hooves in the underbrush was the only sound to be heard, save the occasional chatter of the grouse, or the lowing of cattle in the distance. He didn't blame her for being angry, but the situation wasn't hopeless. When he'd bent her over his knee and smacked her bottom, she had responded to him ever so subtly. He'd win her back.

The hard way, if necessary.

***

The castle came into view just before nonce. The bells from the chapel tolled the hour as the massive stone structure grew large before her. Five stories high, the keep was smaller in width than her own family's home, but twice as high. A short distance from the tower was the beginnings of further construction.

"Castle Ruthven," Blair announced quietly. "I have started planning for a second tower, as well."

Susanna said nothing and refused to turn around. She wouldn't give him the satisfaction of knowing that she was, in fact, quite impressed.

How could he have done this to her? To what end? Mary had always said that men were foolish, but she'd had no idea. To think she'd almost bared her entire heart to the bastard, and not once had he been honest with her. What would he have done if she'd voiced her desire to run away with him and hide from...well, *him*? Would he have laughed? And she'd nearly...

No. Do not think on it.

She regretted having declined her father's offer to teach her swordsmanship because she wanted very much, at the moment, to run her Scottish fiancé through. He likely still would not know what it felt like to have his heart torn from his chest and stomped upon, but it might make *her* feel somewhat better.

Yet, even now, she wanted him. The warmth of his strong body resting against hers, and his hand on her stomach, was distracting her from her silent fuming.

Stop it. You are a Cavendish. Secure by caution. You would do bloody well to remember that from now on.

They were riding down a wide earthen street lined with tiny cottages. People were emerging from their homes and waving to them. Some cheered. Susanna squared her jaw and looked straight ahead, avoiding eye contact with any of them. She heard music drifting on the wind from further down the street, the rolling crack of a drum along with a curious, multi-tonal instrument of some kind that was whiney, yet oddly soothing. *Bagpipes!* she identified with excitement. She'd read of them, and how they accompanied the Scottish armies in the wars. She forced her smile into a scowl, however, determined not to show any happiness or interest.

"Ye'd do well to smile, lass," Blair spoke low into her ear.

"They are your people, your Grace, not mine."

"They are our people now, Susanna," he replied. "An' they have not wronged ye."

A young girl ran up beside their horse and Blair slowed them to match the child's hurried stride. She held up a handful of brightly-colored flowers. "For ye, milady," she declared shyly.

Susanna softened at the innocent gesture. "Thank you." She took the flowers and held them to her nose.

"She's verra pretty, Laird," the girl said.

"Aye, Muireall, she is," Blair replied.

Muireall tugged on the hem of Susanna's gown and motioned with her fingers. Susanna obliged and bent down as far as she was able to without falling face-first in the dirt. Blair's arm, strong and sure around her waist, was probably the only thing keeping her on the horse.

"I like yer hair," Muireall whispered. "Be a good lady for the laird, we like him verra much, and he is'na happy terribly often."

"I will try," Susanna replied in the same hushed tone.

"God bless ye, milady!" the girl cried before running back to her mother.

Damn, Susanna thought with a sigh. *A fine mess I have found myself in.*

***

The inside of the castle was no less impressive than its exterior. If King Henry knew that the Scottish lords lived in elegance that rivaled his own, he likely would not call them heathens. Then again, knowing Henry, perhaps he would. The main hall occupied nearly the entire bottom floor of the keep. A long wooden table spanned its length. Hearths were carved into the stone walls at either end, and above each of them, reaching up almost to the high, painted ceilings, the Ruthven crest was engraved. Brightly colored tapestries, all fashioned in the same plaid pattern as Blair's mantle, hung from the walls at regular intervals. "The clan tartan," he supplied, when he caught her examining the tight weave. "The stories say that the Ruthven ancestors were Vikings who came to Scotland to conquer. My ancestors fought with William Wallace in 1292 to reclaim Perth from Edward the First."

"The Braveheart," Susanna muttered, lured out of her silence by her fascination.

"Aye, Braveheart." He paused and cocked his head. "Have ye read *The Acts and Deeds of Sir William Wallace*?"

She shook her head. "My father could not find me a copy in London."

"I shall lend ye mine," he said. "I think ye would find it interesting."

She looked up at him and smiled. He was giving her books? Her father would never believe it. She would have to write and tell him he'd been wrong...

The smile disappeared and she snapped her head forward again. Blair was trying to win her over, using her biggest weakness. Well, it wouldn't work. She'd accept the book, and she'd read it, but it wouldn't get him back in her good graces. He'd almost opened the door again – now, she had to shut it before he could force his way in.

Her fiancé picked up on her mood shift immediately. He sighed and fell silent once more.

Blair showed her to her bedchamber. His hand, locked firmly around her upper arm, indicated that he expected her to pick up her skirts and run if given the chance. Several women scurried up the stairs behind them, eager to carry out any command, hoping to get another glimpse at the much-anticipated English bride.

Hers was a large suite of rooms, directly across the hall from his own. Beyond her receiving room was the bedroom, and in the center of it was a large, four-poster bed. She could tell, even from the doorway, that the mattress was filled with goose feathers, and she nearly moaned at the sight; a real bed, for the first time in nearly a fortnight. Thank the Lord for small comforts.

A massive hearth spanned the west wall, and to the north was a row of windows – small and deep-set within the thick stone walls overlooking the impressive Scottish countryside.

"This is yer chamber, lass, though after we are married, I should like ye to spend most of yer time in mine." He stood behind her, hands resting on her upper arms.

"I shall do what my Lord requires of me," she responded without emotion.

"I want ye to do what will make ye happy, liuadhe," he said softly.

"If that were true, then I would spend no time in your chambers at all, your Grace."

"Why can ye no be happy with me?" he asked, his voice pained.

"Because you lied to me. I cannot trust you."

"Yer body trusts me," Blair said, stroking her hair. "Yer heart will soon follow."

She closed her eyes and leaned against him. *Step away from him now, or he will trap you again,* she told herself sternly. "No," she spoke aloud, moving forward before turning to face him.

His face darkened. "Dress for dinner, lass," he told her. "I expect to see ye there."

"Please do hold your breath until I arrive, your Grace," she shot back.

He started to respond, then shook his head and, with a sigh, disappeared through the large, wooden door.

There was no way in hell she was going near him if she could help it. She peeled off her gown, climbed into the bed, and slept.

Susanna woke to the sound of someone moving about her room, singing softly in a language she didn't recognize. "Mary," she mumbled, turning her face into the soft pillow, "stop that nonsense and leave me sleep."

"Ye must get up now, milady," a thickly accented voice replied.

Susanna remembered her surroundings and sat up. There was a young girl standing beside her bed, peering at her quizzically. Clear blue eyes stood out amongst a frizzy mess of fiery red hair, framing a pale, freckled face. "Ah, good, yer awake now. Verra good. I dinna want to have to poke ye."

"I...I should like to sleep some more," Susanna stammered, watching as the girl scurried about.

"Time to get ye ready fer supper, milady," the girl chirped, rummaging through one of Susanna's trunks. Apparently, they had all been delivered while she slept. A neat little stack of them took up the far corner of the room.

"I will not be attending supper."

The girl stopped and stared at her. "Laird's orders, ma'am, I'm to get ye dressed an' ready. The bath is on its way."

"What is your name?" Susanna asked.

"Beathag, milady."

"I am not feeling well, Beathag. Please tell his Grace that I wish to stay in bed and rest."

The young girl snorted. She couldn't have been older than Susanna, but was obviously a good representative of the tough as nails Scottish stereotype. "At least have a bath, milady. An' if ye still feel ill, then I shall speak with th' cook about a remedy."

No sooner had Beathag announced the arrival of a bath, than her door swung open and two men tramped in carrying a large wooden tub. Behind them, a line of boys filed in, each carrying a pail of water, which they promptly emptied into it. Susanna could see the steam rising from the water, and sighed in spite of herself. A real bed and a real bath. Yes, this day was improving.

***

Blair paced the foot of the stairs nervously, much as he had a week earlier, before he'd left to meet his bride. She would come. Surely, she would not embarrass him so severely by refusing to appear at dinner. Not when half the clan was waiting to meet her.

Would she?

He cast a glance over at the table, where most of the seats were already filled. His place at the head of the table was empty, as was the seat to his right, where Susanna would sit, and the seat to his left, which was reserved for his brother. Fortunately, his people had started celebrating early in the afternoon -- as soon as word of his return had spread throughout the castle and the town -- and many were too inebriated to pay him much attention.

His father's best friend and trusted advisor, Ian, caught his gaze and gave him a dour smirk. The man had been strongly opposed to the marriage, predicting that no good could come from a union of any kind with the English.

Blair gave Ian a hard stare and then turned his back. He respected the older man, but he was in no mood to hear a lecture tonight.

"Yer Grace?"

He whirled around to see Beathag standing on the stairs, several steps up. Her fingers were playing with the hem of her apron. *Damn...* "Aye?"

"She willna come down, yer Grace." Wide blue eyes darted back and forth as she waited for him to reprimand her.

"Did she say why no?"

"Aye, yer Grace, she says she doesna feel well. I tried. I even had Cook brew her some remedy, but she willna drink it."

"Run along an' get yerself some food, lass. I shall see to her myself." He started to move past her on the stairs.

"Yer Grace?"

"Aye?" he glanced over his shoulder.

"She is verra pretty, yer Grace. But also verra sad. I hope ye can change that."

He stalked up the stairs, trying to calm his temper before he reached Susanna's chambers. Yelling at her would get him nowhere. He was smart enough to realize that. And, though he didn't like the idea, he *had* messed things up rather badly between them, so perhaps some groveling was in order as well...later. A man could only make so many changes at once, after all, and he felt like the wind had been permanently knocked out of him ever since Susanna had stepped into his life. He shouldered open the door to her chamber and stopped in his tracks.

She was standing by the window, looking down over the valley below. Her long, curly hair was loose, the way he liked it, spilling over her shoulders in soft waves. Her satin gown was pale yellow, with a tight bodice and low neckline that displayed the tops of her breasts in all their soft, round perfection.

Why was he angry again? It was hard to be cross with her when she looked so delectable.

"Here to give me more orders, your Grace?" she queried bitterly. "Or perhaps to tie me up and carry me down to the hall? A fine impression that would make."

"I dinna plan to carry ye, lass, though it is tempting."

"Well as I told Beathag, I am not feeling well, and I have had a long journey. I do not think it unreasonable for me to want half a day's peace before you begin to parade me around in front of your people like a captured peacock," she gestured to her ornately hewn gown.

"I want ye to be happy," he said. *Blast, why did she make everything so bloody difficult? And who knew an English lass could be so damned stubborn?*

"If you truly want me to be happy, Blair, then leave me alone."

"I would like ye to come to dinner, Susanna. Please."

"Is that a request or an order, your Grace?"

"A request. At least consider it," he said, before retreating back into the hallway. He knew he wouldn't see her again tonight, and he winced as her harsh words lanced through him again. He shook his head, squared his shoulders, and returned to his guests.

***

Susanna pushed open the door and peered out into the corridor. Damned if she was going to just wait for him to come back and forcibly drag her down the stairs. He could come looking for her, and she knew he would, but she didn't plan on being there when he did.

Susanna fled down the hallway, looking back repeatedly in case he was coming, and slammed straight into a wall. No, not a wall, she realized, as she took in the broad, muscular expanse of male chest. Her gaze rose higher. In the dim torchlight of the passage, she could just barely make out the long, brown hair and well-defined chin. It was him. "Son of a whore!" she cursed.

"I beg yer pardon, lass," he said, "I dinna believe ye know me well enough to call me that."

She damn sure didn't. She knew every inch of his cock, and every nuance of his tongue, but that was where her familiarity ended. She began to tell him as much. *Wait.* She leaned closer and squinted. It wasn't Blair, though this man was a very good facsimile. She smelled liquor – something strong and pungent – on his puff of exhaled breath. "Who the hell are you?"

"Ceallach," he said smoothly, "and yerself?"

Ceallach. Blair had mentioned him to the peasant woman, Ruadh. "An errand boy for the Duke, are you?"

He snorted. "He wishes. My brother doesna have nearly that much control over me, lass."

"Your brother seems rather fond of controlling everything."

"Aye, he is," Ceallach laughed again. "And since I canna imagine a lass such as yerself would have escaped my attention for so long, ye must be his bride."

"Unfortunately."

His laughter doubled. "Ah, lass, I like ye already. Anyone who can peg my brother for the uptight ogre that he is, is alright with me."

" 'Uptight ogre' is a rather generous classification," she responded with obvious bitterness.

"Is it now?" he lifted one eyebrow casually.

God, they are almost identical. "Indeed. I prefer 'amoral, classless, selfish son of a swine'."

"Ye may insult my brother as much as ye like, milady, but our mother was a decent woman, I'll have ye know."

"You are drunk," she stated, taking a step backwards and placing her hands on her hips.

"Sadly, no. But workin' on it." He looked at her for a moment before smiling. "Care to join me?"

"I am supposed to be in the hall for dinner."

"Aye, me too. But I much prefer a smaller party."

Susanna had a feeling her fiancé would not approve of her drinking with his brother like a tavern wench. With any luck, it would make him livid. She returned his smile. "I would love to."

He offered her his hand and, after she'd accepted it, led her down the hall.

"Where can we go?" she asked. "I do not wish to see him, and he is likely to come looking for me."

"I do no care to see him either," he commented with a snicker. "Come with me."

Ceallach led her to the kitchen and left her at the door while he darted inside, returning several moments later with two large flasks of whiskey and two clay cups. Then he led her up a winding flight of stairs to the third floor of the castle, through a small, empty chamber, and down a dark hallway. At the end of the corridor was a stone bench, carved into the wall. The torches on the walls were few and far between, and they ceased entirely about a hundred paces before the bench. The feeble light they cast did more to obscure Susanna's vision than it did to improve it.

"Here we are," Ceallach announced, dropping unceremoniously onto the bench and patting the space beside him.

"Here? It is in the middle of the corridor."

"Aye, but no one comes up here these days. That there," he nodded towards a dingy wooden door, "was my grandfather's mother's room. It's a haunted room, lass. We'll no be disturbed, I promise ye."

Indeed, there was a thick layer of dust covering the floor. Looking closer, Susanna saw that there were torches on the walls here, but they were not lit.

"Haunted by whom?"

"By a changelin', lass. The elves tried to take my great grandmother, but my grandsire discovered their plan an' threw the changelin' lass into the fire. When the elf died, she burst into flames and her body burst through the roof into the night. Even though my grandsire had the roof repaired, every year on the same night, the hole reappears an' no one kin discover why. So now, we simply do no enter the room at all."

"I do not believe in elves or fairies," Susanna stated matter-of-factly.

"Nor do I, lass. But most of my kin do. So they'll no come in this hallway. Sit down, an' have a drink."

She shrugged and sat down.

Ceallach filled one of the cups and handed it to her, then poured one for himself. He drained the entire cup in one draught, then poured a second and grinned at her.

"I like you better than the Duke," she said.

"We look the same, lass."

"Yes, but you are not rude and boorish like your brother."

Ceallach laughed. "I would pay to hear ye say that to his face."

"I do not believe I've told him exactly that, but I did call him an oaf and a brute today," she offered. "Oh...and a cruel, miserable bastard." She took a long drink and made a face. "This is not the most pleasant tasting beverage I have ever tried."

"It will be after a few more sips."

And, indeed, the taste did improve dramatically the more she drank, though she still could not prevent wrinkling her nose and choking back a gag each time she swallowed a mouthful of the pungent, bitter liquid. Her mood improved as well; with each swallow she found her misery over her situation decreased. She also found herself increasingly attracted to her fiancé's brother, who seemed to have all of Blair's desirable characteristics, and none of his unsavory ones. He seemed brutally honest, which, given her current predicament, was a welcome change.

"Your name is very difficult to say after several drinks of this," Susanna commented with a giggle.

"Ye may call me Kelly," he replied. "Only my brother calls me Ceallach, anyway."

Susanna lifted her cup to her lips and missed. A steady stream of whiskey poured down her front.

"Bloody damn," she swore, watching the liquor trickle down the valley between her breasts.

Kelly watched too. "Ye curse as much as I do," he commented, tracing the line of her curves with his eyes. "I find it rather alluring."

"Some day we should trade favorites," she suggested, refilling her cup. She attempted to drink a second time and, finding herself successful, shot him a triumphant grin.

"I must confess somethin' to ye, lass," he whispered, his words slurred.

"What is it with you Ruthvens and lying?" she sighed, taking another sip of whiskey.

"No, no. It is'na a lie, lass, but a confession." He put a hand on the small of her back. "I expected ye to be fat an' ugly."

"I see. And did I live up to your expectations?"

"Nay." He scooted closer. "I find myself verra jealous of Blàr at the moment."

"There is no reason why you should be," she answered slowly, tilting her head to regard him. Oh yes, one thing the Ruthvens were not lacking was physical beauty.

"He gets to marry ye." His gaze raked over her with obvious hunger.

"He has not done so, yet. I am, at present, a free woman."

Kelly's eyes widened at her implication and he licked his lips. "My bràthair would no be pleased if he were to discover...us."

"I expect not," Susanna smiled coyly. "But I do not plan to tell him." *Though it would serve the bastard right to know.*

"Well if I dinna tell him, and you dinna tell him, how will he know?"

She placed her hand on his leg and let her fingers walk a lazy path up his thigh. "I do not believe he will." She tried to stand, meaning to lead him to her bedchamber – or his – but he caught hold of her waist and pulled her down into his lap with her back to him.

Sweeping her hair out of the way, he kissed the side of her neck. The hand around her middle drifted up to cup her breast. He pinched her nipple through her gown, teasing the tiny nub into a stiff peak. "I must have a taste of ye," he whispered.

The two brothers may have looked nearly identical, but their techniques were entirely different. Blair took his time, barely restrained hunger evident in every caress, every kiss. It excited her, not knowing when she would push him over the edge, or what he would do once he got there. Kelly was far more playful. But his hands told her exactly what he wanted, even as his mouth licked and nipped her throat.

His fingers slipped under the neck of her gown and connected with her breast, tugging at her nipple. She moaned. Dropping her head back on his shoulder, she offered her mouth to him and he captured her lips, biting them gently before invading her mouth with his tongue.

"Your hands are rougher," she commented absently when he pulled away to nuzzle her neck again.

Kelly pulled back with a start. "I'll be damned, he bedded ye already."

"Well," she said with a conspiratorial grin, "not *completely*."

"Lass, please," he groaned. "Spare me the details. I canna have that picture in my head, no matter how pretty ye are."

He pushed her to her feet and spun her around, leaning forward to bite her breast through the silk of her gown. Susanna panted against him, hands tangled in his long, brown hair.

"Are ye wet for me, lass?" he asked lewdly.

"Yes," she moaned. She was going to be damned straight into hell for this but, at the moment, she didn't care.

"Do ye want me to lick yer cunny?"

She groaned and arched her back against him. He smacked her ass in response, a stinging slap that she sent sparks straight to her clit.

"Ye like that do ye?" he teased. He pushed her gown from her shoulders and tugged at the neckline until her breasts sprang free of their confinement. Scraping his teeth over one taut nipple, he smacked her again.

She was about to reply when a voice behind them cut through her drunken, lust-filled haze.

"Ceallach, I dinna ken what possesses ye to humiliate yer women by para..." the voice trailed off, all amusement draining from it as Susanna raised her head to identify the intruder.

Blair froze at the sight of her. His eyes were bloodshot and he swayed on his feet, an indication that he, too, had sought to drown the day's memories at the bottom of a whiskey flask. She scrambled to her feet, hastily pulling her gown up over her exposed flesh. Kelly also stood.

"Bràthair, it is'na what ye think-"

"What I *think* is that ye are fuckin' my woman!" Blair roared.

"Well, okay, perhaps it is what ye think, then, but—"

He was cut short by Blair's fist connecting squarely with his jaw. "Get out of my home," he growled through clenched teeth. "I want ye gone by morning. And make yerself scarce until then, *bràthair*, because if I see ye, I will kill ye."

"Blair," Susanna interjected. "Please."

His eyes focused on her. His jaw worked as if he was going to speak, but instead, he crossed the corridor in lengthy strides and picked her up in his arms.

"Blair, put me down! You are drunk!"

"So are ye, my Lady," he growled, "And I will do nothin' of the sort."

Then, for the second time that day, she found herself flung over his shoulder as he carried her down the hall, leaving his brother a sprawled heap on the stone floor.

Chapter Nine

He carried her back to her bedchamber that way, dangling from his broad shoulder like a sack of grain. The sudden rush of blood to her head, combined with the excessive amount of whiskey she'd drunk, made her feel nauseous. He stomped through the door, kicking it shut with one foot, and tossed her onto the bed.

"Oh lord, I think I shall be ill," she gasped, pressing one hand over her mouth.

"Aye, I expect ye will," he seethed, pacing the length of the room. The muscles between his shoulder blades bunched, restrained fury evident in the heavy stomp of his booted feet, and the way the fabric of his mantle snapped when he turned. "Though whether it be from the drink or my brother's dirty cock I neither ken nor care!"

"I did not—"

"Nay, but ye were about to!" he bellowed. "Or is it yer turn to lie to *me* now?"

She said nothing. He was right, after all. Christ, she'd almost...and if he hadn't come upon them, she would have. Blind desire for vengeance had fueled her words, as the liquor had fueled her lust. And Kelly had accepted her advances. Had, in fact, encouraged them. *Dear Lord, what have I done?*

"Do ye feel better now that ye have taken revenge, Susanna?" he asked, eyes flashing.

"I wanted to hurt you!" she cried.

"And ye did a rather thorough job of it, too," he responded with a sneer. "I have banished my own brother."

"Banish *me*. I made the offer to him."

"Aye, I know ye did. Even Ceallach wouldna be so daft. But if he had not gotten ye so bloody drunk, ye never would have done it."

"You do not know that."

"So ye are tellin' me that ye are a whore, then?"

"If I am a whore, it is because you have made me one." The graveness of the situation had sobered her considerably. But her stomach still warred with her, giving her gag reflexes a healthy workout as she fought the urge to vomit.

He flinched. Teeth clenched, she saw the muscles of his jaw work. His eyes, which only moments before had been fiery and animated, had gone cold and lifeless. "I have never forced ye to yer knees, nor have I humiliated ye or degraded ye as my brother intended to," he said, his voice eerily calm. The sudden tranquility terrified her. "Perhaps that was my mistake."

Get away from him, her instinct screamed. *Run, now!*

Susanna rolled onto her stomach and tried to crawl off the bed on the opposite side, hoping to put it between them. She wobbled on all fours and toppled over, head swimming from the whiskey. Strong fingers wrapped around her ankle and she was yanked backwards, hands bunching in the linens as she clawed for leverage.

Blair flipped her onto her back again and crawled on top of her, pinning her beneath him. With one hand, he held her wrists above her head.

"My brother likes it rough," he growled. "Do ye like it rough, lass? Is that why I canna make ye want me?"

"Stop it," she whispered.

"This," he grasped the neckline of her gown and rent the fabric in two. Her breasts spilled out and he gave one nipple a cruel twist, "is mine."

"Stop it," she said again.

"An' this," he slipped his hand down and cupped the mound of her sex through her ruined dress, "is mine as well."

"*Stop!*"

"Should I take ye now? Is this how ye like to be wooed?"

The *no* stuck in her throat and she choked on a sob. Her fear was tangible – a sour, coppery taste in the back of her mouth. Memories of Spencer's hands on her, of his fetid breath against her cheek, of Mary's lifeless body, flooded her consciousness and she whimpered.

"Perhaps we should simply dispense with yer virginity now. Since ye have told me that ye will never come to me willingly anyway, what does it matter?" He lengthened the tear in her gown, the fabric falling away and exposing her stomach to just below her navel.

"If you do this I shall never forgive you. *Never*! You are no better than the bastard who killed Mary!"

That stopped him. His expression cleared, the color draining from his face, even as the life returned to his eyes. "Susanna," he whispered, tracing a finger down her tear-stained cheek. She jerked her head as if he'd slapped her. "Christ..." He stood and punched the wall as hard as he could.

She heard a sharp 'crack' and saw blood blossoming on his knuckles as he drew his hand back. The skin was gouged away in jagged, asymmetrical holes. Blair looked at his hand, flexed his fingers, and then punched the wall a second time. When he pulled away again, blood trickled down his fingers to the floor, and the grey stone was smeared with it as well.

"I'm sorry, liuadhe," he said, dropping to his knees. "Christ, I'm so sorry."

"Blair," she whispered. She felt his anguish call to her, and her heart ached. Ignoring her fear, she went to him, placing a slender hand on his shoulder.

He turned and pressed his face against her thighs, his hands coming up to grasp her hips.

"Forgive me, Susanna." His grip tightened and his body shook.

"I forgive you." And she did. For all of it. "Why did you not care for me enough to tell me the truth?" she asked softly, brushing his hair back from his temple and smoothing her thumb across his furrowed brow. "Why do you not love me as I love you?"

He pressed his cheek harder against her, and his words were muffled in her gown. "I do love ye, lass. With my entire being, I love ye. If I did no, perhaps I would no have been such a fool."

"But..." she trailed off.

"If ye wish to return to yer father an' break the marriage contract, I shall see ye safely back to Devon,"

Blair told her, his voice weary and resigned. "I will bear the wrath of Henry an' James, an' take their punishment."

She sank to her knees and took his face between her palms, then drew him close – foreheads touching -- his hot and flushed, hers cool. "I do not wish to return to my father," she told him softly.

"After what I've done, how can ye—"

She silenced him with a finger upon his lips. "I wish to stay with you, my Lord, if you still will have me, after what *I* have done."

He lifted his head to meet her eyes, then ran his fingers down her jaw. "I love ye, Susanna," he told her.

She smiled, her tears renewed. "And I you."

He kissed her – chaste, gentle, yet full of raw, pure emotion. She sat down on her heels and let him pull her into his arms, where she belonged. He cradled her to him, his cheek against the top of her head.

"Do we forgive each other then?" she ventured. Later, she'd try to convince him to forgive his brother as well. But for now, she'd take it a step at a time.

"Aye."

"Come to bed with me," she suggested, resting her weight against his chest.

"Liuadhe, ye know I want to," he told her, caressing her hair. "But no yet. Once we are married and ye are my wife, I shall be happy to oblige."

"Just stay with me, then." *Whatever you do, don't leave.* She had grown so used to having him at her side as she slept, she wasn't sure she could manage it without him now. Why was it that whenever she was in his arms the rest of the world disappeared? It was the only place she felt safe anymore.

"An army couldna drag me from ye, lass." He stood and gathered her into his arms, then carried her to the bed. He laid her down and curled up behind her, wrapping his body around hers. Their fingers laced together.

"Blair..." she said timidly.

"Aye, lass?"

"I am still going to be sick."

***

Blair wasn't certain how late it was when he finally woke the following morning. It could have been afternoon for all he knew, but that was fine with him. Susanna was sure to have one hell of a headache when she awoke, so he was more than willing to let her sleep off as much of her hangover as possible.

He'd dozed off and on throughout the morning as she'd slept, nursing his own hangover which, with her nestled against his side, wasn't as bad as he believed it should have been. Beathag had poked her head in at some point, but a stern glance from him had been enough to send her away.

He should be angry with his fiancée – no, he should be livid. But he wasn't. He was only more convinced that Susanna was what he wanted.

She stirred in his arms.

"Good morn, my Lord." She smiled up at him. He couldn't prevent returning it with a smile of his own.

"How do ye feel, lass?" Before they'd fallen asleep the night before Susanna had, indeed, discovered the unsavory side effects of overindulging on his country's favorite beverage. He'd stayed by her side through the entire ordeal. After her stomach had rid itself of its contents and, according to Susanna, half her insides, she'd sworn never to touch the stuff again. It was just one more reason why Blair had no desire to see his brother for a good, long while.

"I feel as if my insides have been torn out and my head has been bashed against a wall. Repeatedly." She squeezed her eyes shut and groaned. "And when did the sun become so damned bright?"

He smoothed her hair and pressed a kiss to her temple. "I shall have Cook brew ye a remedy but, unfortunately, there is no much that can be done."

"Ever?" She groaned again and buried her face against his shoulder, burrowing beneath the blankets.

"It will pass in time."

"Will the shame pass as well?" One bright, green eye slitted open and peered up at him.

"It wasna yer fault, liuadhe."

"No? I—"

He saw the tears beading at the corners of her eyes and hurriedly brushed them away. "Do no do it, lass," he said. "One day I shall tell ye of the things I have done after too much whiskey. Besides, ye know I tend to be daft even when I've no had a drink."

"But I feel so very imprudent now," she said with a frown. "What I nearly did far outweighs your own error."

"I should never have lied to ye, lass," he said.

"Why did you?" Her tone was curious, not accusing, and for that, he was grateful.

"Because I was foolish enough to think ye'd no want me if ye knew who I was. It's no the first time I've been a damn fool," Blair confessed.

"Do you refer to what you happened between you and Kelly?"

"Did he tell ye about it?" He couldn't help it; he stiffened. It hadn't been one of his shining moments – but then again, none of them had done much to be proud of lately, it seemed.

"No, he did not." She was tracing lazy patterns across his chest, curling the scant hairs around her fingertips. "But I imagine something must have happened between you for him to be willing to..."

"I arranged for his lass to marry another."

"What? Why?" She sat up and gaped at him.

"Because she was with child. I didna think he would claim the baby; he'd refused to do so before. So I found her a husband." He sighed and rubbed his eyes with his palm. "Later, he told me that he had planned to marry her."

"But he did not tell you of his intentions before you arranged the betrothal?"

He looked sheepish. "I didna ask him."

"Oh." She took a deep breath and raised her eyes to the ceiling, then shook her head. "It was Ruadh, was it not?"

It was his turn to be surprised. "How did ye ken?"

"Her boy." Susanna's eyes connected with his again. "He looks like you. At the time I had thought, perhaps...but now I realize that he looks like Kelly, as well."

"Aye, he does. My brother told me once that his difficulty wasna that he never loved his women, it was that he loved *all* women. I think he is in love with love; not to mention sex."

"How many children *does* Kelly have?"

"Four that I am aware of." He grimaced, then added, "That *he* is aware of."

"With how many women?"

The grimace became a scowl. "Four." Blair really had been, for the most part, celibate for the past several years; mostly because his brother had already bedded half the women in Scotland, and probably some in England, as well. He found it amusing that Ceallach poked fun at Henry's numerous mistresses, when he likely had a list ten times as long. No, Blair did not think his fiancée was a whore, and he regretted calling her such. His brother, however, was a certified cad. And not the least bit sorry for it, either. He could see it now, the lazy lift of one eyebrow and a casual shrug. *She was more than willing, bràthair, I didna force her.*

"Oh," she said again, and from her expression he could tell she was thinking much the same thing. "And...how many do you have?"

He cupped her cheek. "None, liuadhe, though I hope ye will change that before long."

"Do you?"

"Aye, I canna wait to see yer belly round with my bairns." The thought of it made him smile.

"The wedding...when shall it be?"

"When would ye like it to be?" *How about today?*

Susanna shifted in his arms, bringing one slender leg up to wrap around his waist. His entire body went hopefully rigid and his cock leapt to attention. "Soon." She placed a kiss on the corner of his mouth. "Very, very soon."

"If my lady wishes," Blair croaked, his nobility warring with his passion.

"Oh, she wishes," she replied, her lovely contralto voice, rich and sultry, wrapping around him in a gentle caress.

"Careful, lass, or I'll drag ye to the chapel right now, in yer shift."

"Why is that?" She traced a finger across his collarbone, drew a lazy path along the grooves of his muscles. They shivered in unison.

"Because ye are a vixen," he tilted her chin. "An' I rather like it."

***

It was close to midday when they finally roused themselves from bed. As if on cue, Beathag appeared and began readying Susanna's clothes for the day. Blair donned his shirt and mantle as the girl flitted about the room, pulling garments from various trunks and laying them over the top of the dressing screen that stood in one corner.

"A bheil an t-acras ort?" Beathag said to Blair, speaking in Gaelic. The words flowed together without pause, a gentle, lilting lift at the end. A question, Susanna realized.

"Ceart gu leòr. Tha an t-acras orm," he replied.

"Dè tha thu ag iarraidh?"

Susanna frowned, climbed out of bed and walked towards her dressing screen. It was silly, she knew, but part of her was bothered that she couldn't understand their conversation. "Should I worry that you are speaking unflatteringly of me?" she spoke up, trying to keep her voice light and playful.

Blair caught her hand as she brushed past him and brought her palm to his lips. "She asked if I was hungry, an' I said I am. Then she asked what I wanted."

"Oh." *And why could that not be said in English?*

"Forgive us, lass. We are used to speakin' Gaelic, an' are no accustomed to bein' in civilized company."

"You promised to teach me, remember?" she asked, drifting behind the screen.

"Aye. Do ye still wish to learn?"

"Of course." Susanna tossed her dirty shift over the top of the screen and Beathag promptly whisked it away, leaving a clean garment in its place. Her ruined dress from the night before was dropped to the floor. She frowned at it.

"What would ye like to wear today, milady?" Beathag interrupted.

"I liked that dress ye wore last night," Blair suggested.

Susanna was somewhat shocked that neither he nor Beathag saw anything wrong with him lounging in her room as she dressed. Such things simply were not done in England, even when the couple *was* married, which of course, they were not. She peeked around the corner of the screen. "Yes, I liked it too," she replied, holding it up for him to see. The jagged tear down the middle gave evidence that it was a, most regrettable, casualty of last night's argument.

She saw his face flush and realized he'd forgotten. "Ruadh can mend it. I will send for her. Ye can meet with her this afternoon to discuss yer wedding gown, as well."

"Al right," she agreed, ducking back behind the screen.

"Aye, this one," she heard him say. "It matches her eyes."

Several moments later a dark green gown appeared.

"Your Grace?" Susanna ventured.

"Aye?"

"Why do you not wear the dress of the court?" If he'd been dressed as a Duke when she'd first met him, perhaps she would have recognized him for her husband. From what she'd observed, his manner of dress was no different then that of his people.

"I dinna care for all the frills an' finery, lass. It scratches at my neck."

Susanna giggled.

"Now leave us alone, yer Grace," Beathag interrupted. "I must do her hair still."

"Will ye meet me in the hall for a midday meal, lass?"

"Yes."

"I like her hair down," he said, and she heard the door creak open.

After the door had closed, Beathag gave an amused snort. "I thought Ceallach was th' only one who tore dresses with no regard for the mending."

Susanna blushed. "You say that as if you know from experience, Beathag," she commented.

"Indeed," the tiny girl replied. "Because I do, milady."

"You mean you and Kelly..."

"Yes, me, an' I think every other lass in Ruthven territory."

"Does he have a reputation, then? I'd only heard about the Duke before I came here," Susanna tried to sound nonchalant.

"A well earned reputation, miss," Beathag sighed. "*Verra* well earned."

Oh, this is just disturbing. "But you are just a child!"

Another snort. "I am older than ye think, milady. But it doesna matter now. Ceallach left the castle early this morn and would no say where he was headed, only that he'd no return for some time."

Susanna winced. "Perhaps he will change his mind and return in time for the wedding."

"Aye, perhaps, but yer fiancé an' his brother both are damn stubborn pigs," Beathag said idly.

"You have *no* idea."

***

When Susanna appeared on the stairs of the Great Hall, Blair was instantly at her side, leading her to her seat, just to the right of his. It turned out they'd chosen to eat at a very odd time, sometime between the midday meal and supper, and so they were alone.

As alone as one could be in Ruthven Castle, anyway. People milled about everywhere, some pausing to greet the Duke and his bride, others seeming not to notice them at all. It was strange, for Susanna, to be in an atmosphere so laid back. A few men – obviously not nobility from their dress and manner of speech – addressed Blair by his first name with no regard for formality, thought all were careful to address her as "my Lady". It seemed that, with the exception of Kelly's drunken seduction, only Blair had the privilege of calling her "lass".

She liked that.

All her life, Susanna had thought herself to be an independent, enlightened woman. She still was, of course, but there was something about this place, coarse and unrefined, and about her fiancé, who was equally rugged, that made her want to be his.

And that was the truth of the matter. She enjoyed when he took charge of her, enjoyed his strength and dominance. She would never admit it to him, but when he told her that she belonged to him, she liked that, too.

The head cook came out to speak with them personally, none too pleased that they'd chosen to eat in the middle of the day. A stag was being prepared for the evening banquet and they could not, under any circumstances, have that to eat now, she told Blair sternly, with such indignation that the large warrior actually blushed and lowered his head.

Susanna suggested soup, or leftovers from the midday meal – something simple that would not cause the cook too much grief. This seemed to evoke equal horror in the rotund older woman, apparently known simply as "Cook" by the entire clan. Cook scoffed at the idea, saying that her "laird and lady wouldna eat like filthy, starving pigs" on *her* watch, and disappeared once more into the kitchen.

"My goodness," Susanna whispered, wide-eyed, after they'd been left alone again. "She would not last one hour in Henry's kitchen. That man eats morning, noon, and night, and all manner of everything, as well."

Blair laughed. "She has been in charge of the kitchen here since before I was born. I remember when I was a wee bairn, I would try to sneak into the kitchen an' steal swees from the tables. When she caught me, an' she always did, I'd get a flogging so bad I'd no sit down for two days."

She looked at him with horror. "And your parents allowed her to do such a thing?"

"Aye, of course."

"I do not know if I want her alone with our children, milord," she whispered, leaning forward to avoid being overheard. "Ever."

At that, he laughed so hard that she saw tears bead in the corners of his eyes.

***

Despite her protestations, Cook provided a lavish feast of traditional Scottish fare, stating rather dourly, as she shuffled to and fro, that Susanna was far too thin and could never survive a Scottish winter with no meat on her bones. But, just before she left them to their meal, she leaned over and whispered something to Blair, in Gaelic, which he later translated as complete approval of his decision.

As they ate, it was decided that the wedding would be held five days later. The bride and groom were both anxious to be married, but protocol dictated they give important guests enough time to attend the nuptials. Messengers would be sent to Edinburgh and London inviting both courts to attend. The English king would not receive the message in time, which was deliberate, though both Susanna and Blair doubted he would come, regardless. James was equally unlikely to appear, but the couple was more amenable to his presence than to Henry's. The Murrays and the Robertsons would receive invitations, as would the MacGarrys and the Loughlins.

"Your Grace?"

"Aye, my Lady?" His eyes sparkled with amusement at the formal tones they were using. Their relationship, thus far, had been anything but. Hell, chances were good his clan thought they'd already consummated their betrothal. He knew his friends and family members – everyone in the castle was a Ruthven in some form or another – wouldn't judge them for their familiarity, but Susanna seemed concerned with keeping up appearances.

"May I have Beathag as my handmaid?"

He grinned. "I thought ye'd like the lass."

"I do. She reminds me of..."

"Aye, I ken." His fingers brushed her knee beneath the table.

"I have another request."

"Ye are full of wants today, Madame," he teased.

"I suppose I am."

"An' I am more than willing to oblige. What else do ye require?"

"I would like a traditional wedding ceremony," she declared.

His shoulders drooped momentarily. "Of course. We will send for a priest from England." He'd been hoping...well, he would do whatever was required to make her happy, that was what mattered. Though England had recently adopted Protestantism under Henry's rule, and some of Scotland was following suit, his country was, for the most part, still Catholic. He knew that Henry was strictly enforcing conversion upon all his subjects, but had thought that most were still rebelling against the change. But if this was what his bride wanted...

"I meant *your* tradition, milord."

Blair didn't bother to hide his surprise. He took her hand and laced their fingers together. "Ye want a Scottish wedding?"

"Well, I am in Scotland, marrying a Scottish Laird, am I not?"

"A true Highland wedding is in Gaelic, liuadhe," he cautioned, abandoning the formal "my lady" in his happiness.

"Good. I will learn."

It was the third time she'd expressed an interest in his native tongue, but the notion still amazed him. "Beathag will have to teach ye the words."

"You do not wish to teach me yourself?" she pouted.

"I do, but as soon as we say them to each other, we'll be married."

"Oh. Without a father?"

"Have ye heard of handfasting, lass?" he asked, giving her fingers a squeeze.

"A little. I did not think it was done anymore."

"My parents didna have a church ceremony. They were fasted instead," he revealed. His parents had loved each other fiercely. His mother, Anna, had been Murray, and had sacrificed everything to be with his father, inciting a rivalry between the clans in the process. It was one Blair still dealt with.

"Did they love each other?" The concept was so completely foreign amongst the English nobility that she seemed to have difficulty with it.

"Verra much. I used to think too much."

"Too much? How so?"

"My father waged war against the Murrays for her hand. The clans are still enemies, and likely still will be when our son takes the title." He shook his head and sighed. "I ken my father dinna want to leave me to fight his battle, and the Murrays and we Ruthvens have ne'er been completely at peace, but there'll no be reconciliation between us for a long while now. I must keep the borders patrolled at all times, or they raid our lands an' rape our women."

"Why? Was she promised to one of them?" Susanna didn't flinch at the mention of raids, nor at the notion that their child would be forced to deal with the discord between the clans. She was as strong a woman as he'd ever known.

"She was one of them, lass. The laird's daughter."

"And you thought they should not have loved each other?"

"I did. But now I understand."

"What changed your mind?"

He reached into his sporran and withdrew the tiny locket with her portrait, the one that Henry had sent him along with the marriage contract, and placed it on the table.

"Where did you get this?" she asked, leaning forward and studying the painting. "This was commissioned by my father on my nineteenth birthday."

"Henry sent it to James, who gave it to me." He grazed her cheek with his fingertips. "I thought ye the most beautiful lass I'd ever seen. An' the portrait doesna even do ye justice."

"Well, you have had a most unfair advantage, my Lord. I had nary a description of you when I was informed of the engagement." For a moment he thought she was angry again, but then she smiled, a dazzling flash of white teeth. She pushed the portrait back towards him.

"Would ye like to return it to yer father, liuadhe?"

"Do you not want it?"

"If ye let me keep it I plan to carry it with me everywhere. If no, I shall have another made." He winked at her.

"No," she picked it up and set it into his palm, curling his fingers over it. "It seems you are meant to have it."

He kissed her knuckles and slipped the portrait back into his sporran.

"Should we not invite the Murrays to the wedding?" she asked, concern evident in her voice. "I suggested it because they are neighbors, but I was not aware of the tension between you. Perhaps it is a foolish idea."

"We are damned if we do, an' damned if we do no, lass," he sighed. "If we dinna invite them, they will take it as a slight, an' if we do, they'll take it as mockery."

"Goodness," she shook her head. "How very complicated your politics are."

"It is'na politics. Most of these rivalries are blood feuds going back centuries. Sometimes over land-- more often over a lass. We canna remember what started them, only what has fueled them for the last decade or so." He gave a wry smile. "I suppose that is why ye think us barbarians, no?"

"Countries have fought wars for much the same reasons, your Grace. Paris sparked the Trojan War when he fell in love with Helen. And my king made an enemy of Rome for a woman – one whom they now say has lost his favor. It has not been two years since he married Queen Anne, and already his gaze wanders." Her nose scrunched in disgust, as if she'd smelled something foul. "No, you are not barbarians, merely human."

"I thought all the English loved Henry," Blair commented, taking a bite of his lamb.

To his surprise, Susanna actually snorted. "Henry is a fat, selfish old bastard," she proclaimed before spearing a slice of meat with her knife and dropping it onto her plate. "And he thinks with a very specific portion of his anatomy."

Several men, who had been passing through the hall, stopped and gaped at her openly before bursting into laughter.

The knife fell from her hand, which flew to her mouth, and she jerked in her seat, taking notice of the men for the first time. He could see the blush spreading along her hairline and out across her cheeks. "Oh no," she moaned softly.

"Yer Grace," one of the men – his cousin, Edward – said with a bow to Susanna, "I had no idea that yer bride was so thoroughly charmin'. No wonder ye've kept her under lock an' key since yer return."

"Oh no..." Susanna repeated.

He hid a smile. "Edward, stop acting like a ruffian an' come introduce yerself to the Lady. Edward, the Lady Susanna," he announced as the young man sauntered forward and dropped to one knee.

"Milady, I am most humbled to meet ye," Edward said honestly. "An' I sincerely hope ye can keep my wayward cousin in line. Edward Ruthven, at yer eternal service." He placed one hand over his heart in dramatic gallantry.

"I fear it is I who must be kept in line, Edward," Susanna responded, some of her blush fading, "as I should not have made such an uncouth statement about my sovereign king in public."

Ian, who had been watching the exchange closely, gave a short, mirthless laugh. "We've no love for the English pig here, milady. The less ye admire Henry, the more we shall admire ye."

"Perhaps so, but speaking out of turn about one's leader is nothing but foolish. In England, men are found guilty of treason for less."

"Aye, but there are places where a person may speak freely," he offered, arching one eyebrow and crossing his arms over his chest.

"Where?" Her chin lifted slightly.

"Scotland." Ian gave Blair a nod, bowed to Susanna, and then turned and strode through the large wooden doors out into the sunshine. The rest of the men followed.

Once they were gone, Susanna flashed him a lopsided smile. "That went well."

***

That afternoon, Blair showed Susanna the castle. She found herself thinking that it was an appropriate home for the Scottish Laird – large and imposing. Yet, when one looked closely, there was beauty hidden in every corner, richly painted ceilings in intricate Celtic designs here, expertly woven tapestries there. It seemed a ridiculously fanciful and romantic notion, even to her, but it made her smile. She was in love, and though the realization had been startling the night before, drunk and incoherent as she'd been, she embraced it now. Only the Lord knew how long her happiness would last, but she'd be a fool not to enjoy it while she could.

She lost track of the names of those he introduced her to. It seemed that a Ruthven or three lurked around every corner and behind every door of the massive castle. All of his people were welcome in his home at any time, he told her.

Their reactions to her varied, from warm and friendly, to wary and suspicious, to openly hostile.

The library was magnificent, a room as large as the great hall. Books lined every wall, and some sat on tables in the center of the chamber.

She couldn't prevent a happy sigh at the sight of so many books – her father's library was only half as large. She had never seen this many volumes, not even in the king's library.

Blair walked to one of the tables. She followed him absently, eyes roaming over the various titles that she passed. *There are more books here than I could read in a lifetime...*

"Here is the book I spoke to ye about," he said, handing her an intricately bound tome.

"The book on William Wallace?" She took it and looked at it incredulously. "You still wish to lend it to me?"

"Of course. Ye thought I only offered it to win yer heart?"

"No, certainly not!" she scoffed. *That is precisely what you thought, you traitor*, her heart whispered. To cover her embarrassment, she carried the book over to a small settee decorated in velvet fabric of gold, red, and green. She opened the book and began to read, glancing up to smile at him gratefully.

He was staring at her, and making no attempt to be subtle about it.

"What are you doing?" she asked, uncomfortable beneath his intense gaze.

"Memorizing yer face," he replied. "In case ye have been a dream all along."

Chapter Ten

Time raced forward. The following day, Ruadh arrived at the castle, her little boy in tow. Susanna's breath still caught each time she saw the lad – he truly was the spitting image of Kelly, though his angelic smile yet lacked the devious undertones of his father's.

Susanna was a bit standoffish with the young peasant woman when she first appeared to provide her services – more out of shame for her own actions than anything else. She couldn't help it. She had, after all, nearly gone to bed with the father of Ruadh's child. She did not speak of the matter with Blair; in his opinion, the issue was closed, and the less he was reminded of the sight of his fiancée between his brother's knees, face inches from his cock, the better. The one time she'd broached the subject with him, he'd stiffened and replied that the sooner she repressed the entire incident, the sooner he'd be able to do the same.

But after several hours of working with Ruadh to design her wedding gown, she found she could no more prevent herself from liking the woman than she could prevent her shame. There was a genuineness to the petite Scottish lass that Susanna appreciated and admired. And in a perverted way, she began to feel a kinship with Ruadh.

On their third day together, Susanna discovered that Ruadh could read a little. She had been browsing through one of the books from the library while Ruadh moved around her in circles pinning the hem of her gown, when she noticed that the peasant girl was taking peeks at the pages when she passed by.

"Can you read this?" Susanna had asked, startled.

"N-nay, no really, milady," Ruadh'd answered shyly.

After some prodding, it was revealed that she could read about half of the words on the page, albeit clumsily and slowly. Susanna decided that she would teach her to read the rest; it was something she'd always planned to do with Mary.

Blair doted on the little boy, whose name was Fergus, after his grandfather, and it warmed Susanna's heart to see him so gentle, so kind.

The "boys" as Susanna and Ruadh took to calling them, would spend the mornings practicing swordsmanship, which entailed battling each other with sticks to save an imaginary maiden in distress. The afternoons they spent riding, patrolling the land and offering help to the peasants who required it. At supper, they recounted their tales, with Fergus standing on the table and speaking in a voice that was quite regal for a lad of four. Ruadh would watch with rapt attention, eyes glistening with motherly pride. Blair's expression, typically unreadable and impassive when in a large crowd, would soften, and he would cheer and clap at all the appropriate spots – when Fergus described how he'd slain the evil dragon and saved the town, or solved the mystery of the dying crops and provided food for all – and the others present would follow his lead.

It seemed to be an open secret that Kelly was Fergus' father. There were very few things that were actual secrets amongst the clan, Susanna realized, though Kelly's most recent exile was not public information.

Blair slept in Susanna's room each night, strong arms holding her close, and dreamed of children who had his eyes and her smile. They remained celibate, save for the occasional kiss, though the temptation to succumb to her need for him was ever-present in her mind. Their bodies reacted any time they were close.

It was all she could do to keep from jumping him like an alley-cat each time they found themselves alone. Honestly, who would comment if they had a child born three days shy of their nine month anniversary? Did it really matter?

The night before the wedding, Susanna was sitting by the hearth reading *The Acts and Deeds of Sir William Wallace*. Blair lounged next to her, with his head resting in her lap. She was stroking his forehead, and occasionally she would read a particularly fascinating passage aloud to him and ask if he knew anything more about whatever particular event the author was describing.

"Fergus has the makings of a great leader," she mused.

"Aye, he's a strong lad. A good lad."

"Could he ever hold title? As your brother's son?"

"If Ceallach were to acknowledge him, it might be possible, though I doubt he'd ever be more than simple gentry. Even if I died with no heir, the king would never make a bastard Laird or Duke."

She caressed his cheek. She knew he wished there was more he could do for the boy. "Sir William Wallace earned his title, did he not?"

"Aye."

"Well then," she leaned down and kissed his nose.

"I dinna wish the lad to lead a revolt, Susanna, simply to earn a title."

"No, of course not. I merely meant...oh, hell, I have no idea what I meant. It just does not seem fair." She sighed and set the book down beside her.

"Ye have the jitters then?" he peered up at her with concern.

"Yes...and no," she confessed. "I am not nervous to marry you, but to have the responsibility of being your wife, and winning over your clan..."

"Ye've already won them over, liuadhe," he kissed her palm. "As easily as ye won over me."

***

The ceremony was to be held outside, by the loch near the castle. Blair had planned on using the chapel on the grounds, but Susanna had surprised him yet again by asking to have the wedding outdoors, saying that the countryside was too beautiful to not be appreciated. The entire castle was a flurry of nervous energy as they prepared for the wedding, and the celebration feast that would follow. Early in the morning, the Robertsons arrived, and shortly after, the Loughlins and the McGarrys showed up. King

James did not attend, as Blair had predicted, but he did send several emissaries with his blessings, and a small army of servants to help in the kitchen.

Susanna was whisked away just after their morning meal, and Blair was told that under no circumstances was he permitted to see her before the wedding. He greeted his guests, paid a visit to the cook in the kitchen, and then took up his new favorite pastime of pacing. He was in the library, the Great Hall having been overrun by guests and clansmen preparing for the wedding the way all Scottish events were prepared for, with large quantities of whiskey. His pageboy, William, had finally returned from Edinburgh – Blair had actually forgotten he'd left the boy there – and had laid out Blair's clothing, and prepared his bath, happy to be at home and useful again.

It had taken the Scottish Laird less than an hour to bathe, shave, and dress, and now he had nothing to do but wait. He wore his finest mantle, with a fresh, clean undershirt, and a brand new pair of stockings, woven from silk by Ruadh's sister, Ceaththea, who was nearly as skilled a seamstress as Ruadh. His broadsword smacked against his right thigh as he walked, drumming an insistent tattoo that matched the pounding of his heart. Fastened to his left hip were his sporran and sgian dhub.

"Do ye plan to plow a path into the ground, yer Grace?" Ian asked, appearing in the doorway.

"Not intentionally, Ian, but if it happens, it happens," he replied with a shrug.

"This lass has ye all in knots, Blàr, an' I dinna ken why," he crossed his arms and leaned against the frame.

"Because she is the most amazing creature I've ever known? Because she's to be my wife?" Blair stopped pacing and glared at him. He had a feeling he was not going to enjoy this conversation, and he was in no mood to argue with the perpetually sour and pessimistic older man an hour before he went to the altar.

"Aye, she's charmed everyone it seems."

"Everyone but you, Ian."

Ian shrugged. "I am a cynic, yer Grace."

"Ye shouldna be. Ye served my father for years."

"Aye, an' I saw the clan near destroyed when yer father fell for a woman," he stated flatly. "This time, though, ye've no taken a woman from a warring clan, ye've taken one from a warring country."

Blair's jaw ticked. "If ye are tryin' to anger me, Ian, it's working."

"Why is yer bràthair no here for yer wedding, yer Grace?"

"Ceallach made his choices."

"Aye, and ye have made yers." Ian turned and strode from the hall.

Blair swore under his breath and resumed his pacing. If there was anything worse than a cranky old Scottish man, he didn't want to know about it.

"Milord! Milord!" A breathless William saved Blair from further misery by bursting through the door. "It's time, milord. I was sent to fetch ye!"

Thank the Lord for small favors, he thought. "Has everyone gathered, William?" He clapped the boy on the back and strode toward the door.

"Aye, milord!"

"Good job, lad." He walked to the castle entrance with a hand resting possessively on the lad's shoulder.

William was a good boy, he'd never understand why...*Damn.*

He hadn't warned her. In all honesty, he'd forgotten. He would tell her after the ceremony, of course, but he knew her, knew she'd see the resemblance instantly. At least they'd already had the discussion about his brother's wanton behavior, so she wouldn't make the mistake of thinking that the boy was *his*, rather than another of Kelly's bastards.

Right on cue, William piped up. "Milord, will Lord Ceallach be here today? I heard he was no in the castle."

The boy had never been told who his father was, but by some unfortunate instinct, William seemed to know anyway. He worshiped Kelly, even more so than he worshipped Blair. And that was the one thing that bothered him about having banished his brother.

"Nay, lad, he is on an important mission."

"Against the Murrays?"

"Aye." What the hell, a little lie wouldn't hurt.

"Och now..." William breathed.

They reached Blair's stallion, which was waiting for him outside the castle doors. He swung up into the saddle and leaned down to tousle the boy's hair.

Blair rode out to the small loch, just beyond the castle gates, in silent contemplation. Damned if he wasn't nervous, yet again. But she'd gotten under his skin in a great way. She was intelligent, beautiful, charming. Also stubborn, infuriating, antagonistic – more or less his perfect match. He grinned.

The glassy surface of the water came into view. Lord, there were a lot of people gathered – it seemed his entire clan, along with at least half of the Loughlins, Robertsons, and McGarrys had shown up.

They were gathered around in small groups as they waited for the ceremony to begin. Someone caught sight of him and cheered. The boisterous greeting spread through the crowd as he rode to the front and dismounted before the priest. William was at his side to lead away the horse, and then returned after he'd secured the animal not far away.

"She'll be comin' shortly, milord," he announced in a nervous whisper.

Blair's breath caught as she appeared over the hill, astride a large, snow-white steed that he'd never seen amongst his stables before.

"A gift from the king for the Lady," William whispered, clearly pleased at having kept a secret from his laird.

"Forget the stallion," Blair muttered in return. "Look at *her*." He glanced at the sky. It was still early afternoon. He had to wait...how long to get her out of that gown? Blast. It was going to be an uncomfortable evening.

Susannah's dress was entirely gold, with stitched embroidery along the waist, neckline, and hem. Her neck and shoulders were bare, the sleeves beginning just below her shoulder and stopping at her wrists, where her hands were covered by puffs of delicate white lace. The torso of the dress was corseted, tapering into a point at her waist where the skirt flared out from her hips. Her breasts were high and full, the rounded tops peeking out from the neckline in wicked temptation.

Her headpiece was simple – she had been rather adamant about her dislike for the latest fashion in London, inspired by Queen Anne's time in France, preferring an austere golden cap with a long, sheer veil.

The horse, being led by the very capable and overly boisterous Fergus, came to a halt just before him. Blair stepped forward and helped Susanna dismount, his hands lingering on the delicate curve of her hips for one tantalizing moment before he released her and offered his palm. She allowed him to lead her before the priest, who stood on the banks of the loch, the rose petals were strewn around them in a makeshift aisle and altar.

She stiffened momentarily, when she caught sight of his pageboy, casting a brief, wide-eyed stare at Blair before regaining her composure and turning back to face forward again. William bowed to Susanna and then scurried off to stand in the crowd.

The priest cleared his throat and the crowd, reluctantly, fell silent. Blair didn't pay attention as the elderly man expostulated on marriage, life, death, God, sin, and pretty much everything he could think of. He watched Susanna, who was doing her best to remain attentive, but looked decidedly bored. His need to touch her was overwhelming, and he began to think of the vilest things imaginable, willing away his erection and the desire to throw her onto his horse and ride away into the woods where he could have his way with her.

Vomit...lots of vomit. Rotting meat. Stale milk. Castration. At that his groin clenched in protest. *Castration...aye, ye heard me.*

"Ahem," the priest gave him a dour look. "Yer Grace, yer vows?"

Well, that worked. He turned to face Susanna and took both of her hands in his. Beneath her veil he could see a glint in her eye that told him she had a rather good idea of what his problem was.

"Tha mise, Blàr, a-nis 'gad ghabhail-sa Susanna gu bhith 'nam chèile phòsda," he recited, squeezing her hands for emphasis and giving her an encouraging smile. "Ann am fianais Dhè's na tha seo de fhianaisean tha mise a'gealltainn a bhith 'nam fhear pòsda dìleas gràdhach agus tairis dhuista, gus an dean Dia leis a' bhàs ar dealachadh."

The priest smiled and nodded to her. She took a deep breath and recited her own vows.

"Tha mise, Susanna, a-nis 'gad ghabhail-sa Blair gu bhith 'nam chèile pòsda. Ann am fianais Dhè's na tha seo de fhianaisean tha mise a'gealltainn a bhith 'nam bhean phòsda dhìleas ghràdhach agus thairis dhuitsa, gu an dean Dia leis a' bhàs ar dealachadh."

Blair beamed at her. Her Gaelic was smooth and clean, though slightly unrefined. It was obvious that she was not a native speaker, but he was confident she would learn very quickly.

The couple turned back to the priest, who resumed his expostulation; Blair resumed his noxious internal recitations until, eventually, the ceremony was concluded.

"I present to you the Duke and Duchess of Perthshire," the Priest announced with flourish. The crowd roared.

William reappeared with his Laird's horse, and Blair helped Susanna into the saddle before swinging up behind her. They rode back towards the castle with the guests close behind, intent on beginning the celebration.

"Ruadh did a fine job on my dress, I think," she gave him a sideways glance. "Do you not agree?"

"Aye, perhaps too fine a job, my Lady."

"Too fine?"

"Aye." He leaned in close and whispered against her ear, "I find myself counting the moments until I kin take it off ye."

She pressed her hand to her mouth to suppress her giggle and bowed her head to hide her blush. "You are horrid!" she hissed.

"Agreed, lass."

As soon as it was dark, Blair stood and announced his intent to take his wife to his bedchamber. They were met with the requisite ribald laughter and drunken encouragement as he lifted her from her chair and carried her up the stairs.

He didn't care. He was done waiting. She was finally his, and he planned to have her.

Beathag, Ruadh, and several other women rushed forward, intent on readying Susanna for the night, but he shook his head at them, fighting back the urge to growl.

"This is becoming a habit, your Grace," Susanna commented.

"What is, lass?"

"You carrying me places."

"Aye, well, this time ye are no over my shoulder," he smiled at her and quickened his pace. Had his castle always been so large? He could swear the damn thing was larger now than it had been yesterday.

"At long last," he muttered when the doors to his bedchamber came into view. He pushed the door open with his shoulder, stepped into the room, and kicked it shut again.

She giggled when he set her down, a high delicate sound.

"I have something for ye, lass," he said, reaching into his sporran. He produced a ring – a small golden band with an intricate knotwork design engraved on the outside. On the inside was a phrase written in Gaelic, *cuirle ma choide.* "Scottish gold," he explained, slipping the ring onto her finger. "So there can be no mistaking that ye are mine."

"What does it say?" she twisted the band around her finger, enjoying the feel of the cold metal.

"Pulse of my heart," he supplied.

Her smile blinded him. "Thank you. It is beautiful."

"It belonged to my mother. My father had it made for her, before they married. He had Ian carry it to her in secret, the night before her brother's wedding. He sent the message that if she wore it, he'd ken she wanted to be his. When he arrived as a guest the next day, she wore it on her finger."

"And then she ran away with him?"

"Aye, that same day."

Susanna sighed and gave him a wistful smile. "How wonderfully romantic."

Yes, it was a romantic story, when one left out the subsequent blood feud. "We have a rather romantic tale ourselves, don't we lass?" He grasped her chin, then dipped his head and kissed her.

"Blair?" she whispered in a breathy voice close to his ear, which she proceeded to give a playful nip.

She wanted to talk? Now? Damn her. "Aye?"

"What shall I call you in public? Laird, or your Grace?" her lips closed around his earlobe again, lingering longer this time.

He groaned. "Ye kin call me anythin' ye damn well please, lass, so long as ye keep doin' that."

"I am serious," she said as she continued to tongue the sensitive flesh.

"So am I."

He felt her tremor. "Are ye frightened, liuadhe?" he asked, nuzzling her cheek.

***

"Perhaps a bit nervous," she admitted, biting her lower lip. Mary had told her once, years ago, that losing one's virginity was quite painful. She'd actually forgotten until Ruadh had told her much the same thing earlier that day. Her husband was a rather large man and...

"I'll no do anything ye dinna wish me to," he said, speaking in that same low, husky voice, ripe with need and passion. His fingers ghosted down her sides and came to rest at the small of her back, pulling her closer. "If ye are no ready, then I will wait."

"But I want to please you," she whispered.

"Ye do, wife." Deft fingers were undoing the laces of her gown and she felt the fabric grow slack around her shoulders, begin to slip down her arms.

She kissed his cheek and whispered, "Tha gaol agam ort." *I love you.*

He pulled back with a start. "Where did ye learn that?"

"Beathag taught me a few extra phrases," she beamed at him.

"And what else did she teach ye?"

"An toir thu dhomh pòg?" she asked softly, offering her lips to him.

"Lass, I shall give ye a thousand." He kissed her, his tongue plundering her mouth in gentle exploration.

She pulled away and smiled at him. "That was one."

Her gown slipped down her bare arms and he kissed her shoulder. "Two," he supplied. He pushed the fabric down over her hips to pool on the floor, kissing each new patch of skin that was bared. Picking her up once more, he carried her to the bed and set her down before unwinding his mantle and joining her on the mattress. His hands skimmed across her torso, palming each breast before he leant forward and took one nipple into his mouth, flicking his tongue lazily over the sensitive nub.

Susanna felt a rush of fluid between her thighs and spread her legs wider, tangling one hand in Blair's chestnut locks.

His large, rough hands drifted lower, stroking her thighs before gliding one finger through her auburn curls.

"Oooh," Susanna sighed, letting her eyes drift closed.

Blair pushed her legs farther apart and positioned himself between them, pausing to inhale the heady scent of her arousal. Then he lowered his head, tracing her already-wet folds with his tongue.

Susanna's hips bucked and she whimpered. Blair took his time, gliding over the sensitive hidden bundle of nerves with long, firm strokes.

She felt a finger slide inside her, and Blair's tongue returned to her clit as he stretched her in preparation for a much larger portion of his anatomy. Her legs began to tremble and she bit back a cry. Just when she felt the first, fluttering contractions of her climax, he inserted a second finger, hooking them upwards to stroke at Susanna's sensitive spot.

"Blair..." she moaned.

"Aye?" He lifted his head to peer at her.

"Please, Blair," she reached for him, tried to pull him on top of her, but he remained firmly rooted between her legs, one large hand stroking her soft skin.

"Do ye remember what I told ye, lass, the night I first kissed ye?" As if to jog her memory, he launched a volley of kisses upon her stomach and inner thighs. "I said I would no take yer virginity unless ye asked me too."

Susanna blushed. Then she let go of her inhibition. Grasping his chin, she met his gaze – her emerald eyes shining. "Will you take me, husband?"

"As my lady wishes," he said.

He kissed his way up her body, taking great care to pay homage to her breasts, which he again declared to be perfect. Her thighs were wet, and she moaned when he rubbed his length along her sex. It pulsed against her clit.

"It will hurt some, liuadhe, but I will try to be gentle," he murmured.

"I trust you," she whispered as she kissed his chin, brushing her lips against the coarse stubble along his jaw line.

His cock nudged against her and he eased just the tip inside. He was watching her intently, studying her face for any signs of discomfort. She nodded and smiled at him, hands resting on his forearms. Then with agonizing patience he pushed into her. Her body expanded to accept him. Susanna felt impossibly full. Deliciously fulfilled.

He stopped when he brushed against her maidenhead and tried to hold still. His shoulders trembled from the effort.

Susanna decided it would be best to get the pain over with swiftly. Before he could stop her, she arched her back, thrust her hips upwards, and sheathed him completely. Her ankles locked around the small of his back, arms tight around his neck, and she held herself there, stubbornly refusing to withdraw even as her eyes filled at the sharp, stinging pain.

"Susanna," Blair gasped, caught entirely off guard. The tremble became a shake as her enticing warmth drew him in.

"It is not so bad," she said. And in truth, it wasn't. The pain had been excruciating for one swift moment, but had begun to fade almost instantly.

"Are ye sure?" he asked in a strained voice. He momentarily lost his battle for control and bucked against her, a quick, shallow thrust out and then back in.

She moaned. Oh, it was quite far from *bad*. It was the most wickedly wonderful thing she'd ever felt. "And getting better by the moment, my Lord." She rocked her hips in a clumsy, but effective rhythm.

"Christ, ye feel good," he groaned.

"Do I?" Heaven help her, she loved it when he said such things.

He withdrew until only the tip of his cock remained inside her, then slid back into her tight heat. Bracing his hands on either side of her, he began a slow, steady rhythm, moving with shallow strokes, as if he still feared hurting her.

She ran her fingers over the straining ridges of his biceps, down the smooth planes of his chest--now covered with a light sheen of sweat--and around to trace the corded muscles of his back.

He bent his head and took one nipple between his teeth, then moved up to lick the column of her throat. When he reached her ear, his tongue swirled inside in a moist caress.

Her breath was coming in soft, shallow pants. Her back arched, breasts proud against his chest. The friction against her straining nipples as he moved above her was creating sensations in tandem with those between her legs.

Another withdrawal, another return. How could she have ever feared something that was so natural, so right? She moaned his name over and over.

Through half-lidded eyes, she saw his expression change, growing fierce and domineering. "Do ye like it, liuadhe?" he asked, lips curling into a lusty, wicked grin.

"Yes! God, yes."

"Do ye want more?"

She nodded, fingers digging into his shoulder blades.

"Say it," he growled.

"I want more."

His eyes went feral, and he increased the force of his thrusts, longer, harder.

Oh, God... She loved it when he lost control. When he stopped worrying about hurting her or offending her sensibilities. It made her feel beautiful – wanted. For all her education and long-ingrained propriety, she loved the warrior in him. She loved it when he dominated her. It was only when he abandoned all restraint that she felt as if she could tame him.

That glorious tension was building inside her again, driving her, and of its own accord, her body found his rhythm and began helping him, hips rising to meet his thrusts, legs fallen wide to welcome him. The vaulted bedchamber echoed with the sounds of lovemaking – raw and visceral. She threw her head back, squeezed shut her eyes, and keened loudly.

"Come for me, Susanna," Blair demanded, and he increased his speed yet again, encouraged by her frantic, mewling cries.

She did. His tone was guttural and animalistic, and it sent her over the edge, careening into the abyss of pleasure with such force that her vision darkened. She felt her muscles contract around him, was dimly aware that he too was climaxing, his seed filling her.

She was a trembling, boneless heap as he rolled onto his side and pulled her into his arms, cradling her head against his chest. She could hear the thundering beat of his heart. Eventually, some of her strength returned and she nuzzled against his shoulder, inhaling deeply of his musky, masculine scent.

"Welcome back, liuadhe," he said.

Her reply was a contented sigh. *Why on Earth had she insisted they wait?*

He seemed to read her thoughts. "The waiting made it all the sweeter, I think," he murmured against her hair.

"I enjoyed that very much," she answered dreamily, feeling the tug of exhaustion on the outskirts of her complete and total satisfaction. She yawned. "I should like...to enjoy it some more, later."

He smoothed her brow and kissed her hair. "I live to please only you, Duchess."

"Blair?"

"Aye?"

"Do you think that was a thousand kisses?"

"I dinna ken, lass, were ye no keeping track?"

"No," she yawned again. "I lost count after twelve."

Chapter Eleven

Airril slumped onto a log and flung the empty wineskin to the ground with a frustrated grunt. He'd be damned if he was going to go back inside and secure more whiskey for himself. No, better to sit out here in the cold and actually sober up than to return to the castle and see *them*. His miserable whore of a wife looked the happiest she'd been in five years, and he had no desire to see her smile, nor to witness *his* happiness.

What right did *he* have to be happy after the agony he'd caused? *She'll make a good wife for ye, Airril. Ye can raise the bairn as yer own an' none shall be the wiser for it.* None, except, of course his entire clan and half of the rest of Scotland. And by 'good wife', *he'd* apparently meant a miserable, cheating bitch.

At least the wedding celebration was providing him a reprieve from his deplorable family situation. His wife had been summoned to the castle to make the English wench's marriage gown, and the little bastard had gone with her. In the past he would have been furious about the laird's directive – his wife staying in the castle meant his wife being close to her lover – but he was beyond caring. He was beyond trying to make her fall in love with him. He was the cuckolded husband, the laughing stock of the clan. And he knew by now, that his status wasn't likely to change.

"Not enjoying the festivities?" a rugged voice spoke up behind him.

Airril whirled around, fumbling for his dirk. He grasped the hilt and waved the small blade clumsily before him. "Who are ye?"

"An enemy...or a friend."

Airril snorted.

"Here," the man limped forward and extended one hand, offering a fresh flask of whiskey. "Why are ye not inside?"

Airril snorted again, but accepted the liquor. "Why are ye no?"

"I wasn't invited."

"Murray." He swore and brandished his dagger again.

The man laughed. "Do I sound like a Murray to ye, boy?"

No, he didn't. The man sounded... "English," he snarled.

"Of that, I am guilty." The man hobbled towards him and sat, with some difficulty, upon the log. "I have no love for yer laird, boy. An' I sense from yer absence at his marriage celebration, that neither do ye."

"I dinna trust the English," Airril said, even as he continued to drain the flask of whiskey.

"Ye do not have to trust me, boy. Only listen."

***

Susanna woke to a dull throb between her legs, and Blair's lips on her skin. Being kissed awake was definitely something she could get used to, she thought, as his mouth traveled down her neck to the swell of her bosom.

"Mmm."

"Good morn, liuadhe," he murmured against her right breast, sliding his tongue over the rosy peak, already a tight little pearl under his attentions.

She reached for him – or at least tried to – but found her hands immobile, wrists securely tied above her with a silken cord, wrapped around both wrists together, then around the wooden framework of the headboard. Her eyes snapped open, and she tugged on the restrains; they weren't tight, but she was held firmly in place.

"Blair?" she asked timidly.

He continued to lave her nipple, teasing the puckered flesh, and gave her a gentle nip with his teeth. One hand trailed a lazy path down her side before slipping between her thighs to cup her sex.

She shivered. "Blair, why am I tied up?"

He paused in his ministrations, raising his head to peer at her through the tangled mess of his braids. The look in his eyes was the same as it had been the night before – lusty, wicked. "I was curious."

"Curious?" she gasped as his long fingers parted the folds of her sex, skimming through her slickness, seeking out her clit.

"Aye."

"What could you possibly have been curious about that would involve tying me to your bed, my lord?" She moaned when he found his target and stroked across the tiny bud with slow, deliberate sweeps of his fingers.

"I was curious about how ye'd look tied to my bed."

Oh. "And are you satisfied?" Susanna bit her lip to stave off another moan.

"No." He rotated his hand, settling his thumb over her clit, and slipped one finger inside of her, probing gently. "Are ye sore?"

"No," she lied. Not enough to ask him to stop, anyway. Her back arched, and she rocked her hips forward into his caress.

"Do ye want me to stop?"

"No!" she exclaimed emphatically, and felt her cheeks flush.

"Ye like what I do to ye, don't ye, lass?"

"Oh, yes."

"Are ye pleased to be my wife?" He continued his tender exploration.

"Mmm, yes."

"An' ye'll never let another man touch ye this way, will ye, liuadhe?"

"No," she moaned.

"Because you're mine." He stroked her harder, faster, coaxing her clit from beneath its hood. Then, without warning, he delivered a sharp smack to her sex with his open palm. Susanna shrieked, pleasure and pain together. She writhed beneath him, torn between pulling away and grinding against him, between wanting him to stop, and wanting more. "Ye like that, too, don't ye?"

"Yes!"

"So passionate," he murmured. He smacked her again.

"Oh God, Blair! Please, I need you," she begged. She twisted against the restraints, her hands tugging against the silk cord in an effort to break free and push forward onto his waiting cock.

He grinned at her. "Turn around, lass," he ordered.

"Why? How?" Now she was confused. Didn't he want her?

"Trust me," he said simply, and rolled her onto her stomach. The cord twisted, but there was enough give to leave her comfortable. It seemed her husband had thought things through rather well, beyond a mere passing curiosity. Blair's hands grasped her waist and pulled her onto her knees. "I havena spent enough time exploring this side of ye, lass," he commented, running one hand over the swell of her raised ass.

Uh oh. That sounded...well, rather interesting, she had to admit. "What are you going to-"

He entered her without warning, pushing fully into her tight heat. He felt even larger from this angle, filling her to capacity. She cried out, expanding to fit him, her muscles clenching his cock, and from his low, guttural moan, she knew he liked it.

Their coupling was primitive, but at the same time sensuously romantic, full of passion, possession, domination.

Blair wound one hand through her long hair and jerked her head back to expose her throat, leaning forward to nip at her neck. "Ye belong to me, lass," he whispered against her ear, punctuating each word with a pump of his hips.

She groaned, rocking her hips back to meet his thrusts, using her restraints for leverage.

His free hand snaked around her body to rub her clit. "Tell me who you belong to."

"You," she moaned helplessly.

"Tell me again," he demanded, squeezing the firm nub of flesh between his thumb and forefinger.

Susanna bucked against him. "I'm yours, Blair, yours!"

"*Again!*" he roared and released her hair, then smacked her ass with his palm.

"*Yours!*" she screamed. Could the entire castle hear them, she wondered? Strange that she didn't care. She was panting beneath him, half-sobbing for air as she continued to climb the peak towards release, his fingers still teasing her clit in swift circles as his cock thrust in and out of her at a slow, steady pace, stroking her sweet spot. Susanna ground against him, urging him faster, harder, desperate to be pushed over the edge. He smacked her again. And again.

She came hard. Her head thrashed from side to side, she shouted his name over and over, milking his release from him, as he continued to pound against her, the rhythmic slap of flesh against flesh barely audible below her keening cries.

Blair withdrew his softening cock and pushed three fingers into her, working her to a second orgasm even more explosive than the first. She felt their mingled fluids, warm and slick on her thighs. The flesh of her rear stung, bloomed as if she'd been pricked by a dozen needles. Her knees gave way and she slid back down to the mattress, his arm around her waist controlling her collapse. Still his fingers worked her, she felt a third climax building.

Oh God, it was too much. Her nerves were tingling, her sex aflame; there was only so much she could take before she lost her mind. "I can't!" she gasped, panting beneath him.

He was unrelenting, continuing to stroke her hypersensitive clit until he was rewarded with another high-pitched wail as she came again.

"Stop," she sobbed, but still he fondled her; almost immediately she felt the tension building again, so intense that it was painful. "Oh God, stop! Please!"

"Ye are so beautiful when ye come, liuadhe. I could watch ye all day."

"I cannot take anymore. Blair, please!" she shrieked.

His fingers disappeared. She moaned, relieved, and let her muscles relax somewhat, still trembling with the aftershocks of her orgasms.

"Susanna," he said, and his voice was close to her ear, stroking her hair.

All she could manage in respond was a muffle groan.

"I think ye *can* take more."

***

When he was a boy, Blair had caught his grandfather sneaking out to the taverns of Perth one evening, seeking the company of one of the local wenches whose charms were available to any with a pocketful of coins. He'd asked, with the curiosity and bluntness of a youngster, why a man would go to a whore when he had a wife at home. "Because, lad," his grandsire had told him simply, "wives are to be cherished. When ye take one yerself, ye must always be gentle with her an' no disturb her modesty. When a laird needs satisfaction, he must find a whore. A woman who would please ye well does no have the breeding to be the wife of the laird."

Blair hadn't seen the sense in that. He especially didn't now, with his wife's supine, naked form shuddering beneath him, her breath coming in soft, shallow pants, her hair fanned out across the pillow in a blazing shock of red curls. She brought out the beast in him – that part of his warrior soul coiled deep within, the part he'd spent most of his life trying to tame and keep dormant. It was the beast that fought on the battlefield, the beast that wielded his broadsword with deadly precision, the beast that had slain Susanna's abductors and scarred the treacherous Spencer for life. And it was the beast that reared its head now, demanded he take her, demanded he possess her completely. Though if he were being completely honest with himself, Blair realized that the man, too, wanted no doubt in his mind, hers, or even his clan who most assuredly heard his wife's desperate, rapturous cries. His forever.

The one thing that the beast refused to recognize was that she was as much his master as he was hers. He would never harm her. His hand fell away from her hair and smoothed the silken curve of her back in a gesture that was both soothing and sinful, ripe with wicked promise. Despite her protestations to the contrary, she raised her ass ever so slightly against his palm, pushing into his caress with the last bit of strength she had. Every part of her was passion incarnate, and he resolved to show her that she could, indeed, withstand more pleasure.

"Kin ye feel my seed inside yer womb, liuadhe?" he murmured, brushing his lips down her spine.

Susanna moaned.

"I see it betwixt your thighs, spiorad càirdeach. It makes me want to fill ye again," He lifted her limp frame and rolled her onto her back once more; his already drenched fingers slipped back inside her, "an' again."

She whimpered. "No more."

"Yes, more." He trailed a moist path up her body and traced her slightly parted lips, before he slipped one finger into her mouth.

Susanna swept her tongue across the pad of his fingertip and she moaned again, sucking away their mingled fluids.

"Good girl," he said with an arrogant smile. So this was what his brother found so appealing about making women beg. Yes, he understood it now. His free hand curled around his cock, coaxing it back to life with swift, firm strokes. His body needed little convincing, his length swelled as his gaze roamed over his wife's limp frame. Her arms still bound above her, hair stringy with sweat, her legs splayed, and the pink folds of her sex glistened in the mixture of candlelight and morning sun, a sacrifice to the beast. Her pleasure and her submission were his aphrodisiacs.

Blair growled and mounted her, his ragged breathing against her cheek evidence of his struggle for control. The beast wanted to take her hard and fast, but the man wanted to go slowly, to love her, to worship her, and most importantly, to make her scream for him once more.

"Look at me," he urged. He pushed his hips forward, bit back another growl at the enticing friction of his length gliding through her slickness.

Her eyes fluttered open, two limitless pools of green. Her gaze was unsteady, but she struggled to focus, to obey him. *To please him.* The innocence in her eyes calmed him, helped to tame the beast. "Would ye like me to untie ye?"

There was a pause, her eyes unclouded some as her strength returned. "No, milord."

Not the answer he'd been expecting, Blair smiled at her and pushed forward slowly, testing his control as her satiny heat drew him in. "I never knew an angel could be a vixen," he murmured. She was tight and warm, like liquid fire wrapped around his cock.

"Do you like it, milord?" she teased, using his words from the night before.

"Aye, little vixen," he grunted, pinching her nipples in turn. She moaned and took his earlobe between her teeth, suckling the tender flesh. God, but the woman learned quickly.

Blair took his time, making love to her at an unhurried, leisurely pace. He wanted to stay like this – inside her, loving her – forever. But it was inevitable that the pleasure would start to build. The walls of her passage spasmed, milking his cock as she came and moments later he joined her, his orgasm washing over him like waves against the shore.

At last he freed her wrists, and collapsed beside her, exhausted. Susanna curled up against his side and lay her head against his chest, one slender leg draped casually over his waist.

"How many ways are there to..." she trailed off, cheeks flushing prettily.

"To make love?" Blair chuckled. "Dozens. An' I plan for us to explore them all."

Susanna sighed. "We do the most wicked things, your Grace, but..."

"Aye, but?"

"But I like it."

***

"I see another pattern developing here, your Grace," Susanna announced as they descended the stairs to the Great Hall late that afternoon.

"What's that, liuadhe?"

"We seem unable to rouse ourselves before midday." Her hand was resting demurely against his bicep, and she kept her voice low.

He chuckled. "I could say something verra crude about that, my Lady, but I will instead assure ye that there is no shame in a wedding night well spent."

She felt her cheeks flush and dipped her head, biting her lower lip. Well spent, indeed. She was making a conscious effort to not walk as if she'd spent a week astride a horse. The throb between her legs was a constant reminder of exactly how they'd occupied the last twelve hours. Her husband had a definite swagger to his own steps, and her blush deepened.

"Are ye alright, my love?" Blair murmured.

She flashed him a smile. "Yes, of course."

They reached the landing and turned the corner on the stairs. Both took in the maelstrom of clothes, bodies, and food that littered the Great Hall – Susanna with unconcealed shock, Blair with dry amusement.

"Good Lord, are they drunk already?" she asked, surveying the crowd. There were people everywhere, slumping over the table, on the floor, half in and half out of chairs. Those not entirely passed out were listing heavily to one side or the other.

"No already, still."

"Oh, my..."

"They may be a bit bawdy, lass," her husband warned.

"You Scots and your..." she glanced sideways at him and found him watching her with a teasing smirk. "...bawdiness," she finished lamely.

"I shall handle it."

One of the men caught sight of them and roused the crowd. The noble couple descended the remainder of the stairs to a bevy of cheers and whistles. Susanna blushed and shook her curls – which she had worn loose at her husband's request – over her face to hide her embarrassment.

"She has the look of a lass well-serviced, yer Grace," Edward yelled.

"Pity yer own woman doesna, lad," Blair shot back and the crowd roared with laughter.

Edward opened his mouth to retort, but the man next to him intervened with a clap on his shoulder. "I wouldna try it, young Edward," he warned. "The laird is'na to be trifled with when it comes to his woman."

Amidst more laughter, Blair led Susanna to the head of the table, seating her to his right before taking his own place. The same boy who had stood by him the day before appeared at his side.

"Milord? What can I get ye?"

"Whiskey for me, William. And for the Duchess..." he lifted an eyebrow at her.

"Wine, please, if you have any."

"No whiskey, milady?" William asked innocently.

"Absolutely not!" she exclaimed, and the poor boy jumped at her vehemence. "I mean I...I have no stomach for whiskey. William, is it?"

"Aye, milady."

"I would thank you for some wine, William."

"Aye, milady!" William called over his shoulder and took off at a run the direction of the kitchen.

She turned back to Blair. "Another of your brother's?"

He nodded. "I took him as my pageboy when he was eight."

William returned, moving at the same breakneck speed. "And now some food, milord?"

"Aye." The boy started to run again. "An' William?"

"Aye?"

"Slow down before ye break yer neck, lad."

"Aye!"

Blair chuckled and sipped his whiskey. "He listens about as well as his father."

Susanna noticed the man who'd regarded her with such disdain – Ian – watching her from the corner of the room. He had the same look of irritation on his face. She smiled at him and his scowl deepened. *Oh, I have had quite enough of this*, she thought.

"Ian, a moment?" Susanna asked politely, lifting her voice to be heard over the din of the crowd.

Ian inclined his head in her direction. "Yer Grace." He took the seat next to her, its occupant having slid onto the floor unconscious some time ago.

"You are not very fond of me, are you?" She took a sip of her wine, tried to keep her tone casual. Oh, her father would have been furious if he'd heard her broaching such a topic in polite company. *Well*, she one again glanced around at the inebriated gathering, *company, anyway.*

"Nay, milady, I am no."

Susanna raised her brow. She appreciated his honesty. "May I ask why?"

"What bothers me, Madame, is'na that ye married him, as I've no doubt the decision wasna in yer hands, but that ye play with his emotions so." Ian scowled at her. "He's been a strong leader, but now he fancies himself in love with ye."

Susanna's jaw dropped. She clamped it shut again, and drew her brows together. How could this man think so horribly of her when he didn't even know her? "Ian, my feelings for his Grace are genuine, whether you believe them to be or not."

"Clearly, milady, I do no."

"Has he told you what befell me on my journey here?" she asked setting down her goblet and turning to face him fully.

"Nay, he hasna spent much time with anyone but yerself since his return."

"I was kidnapped in Northumberland," she supplied. "My entire guard was killed, even the one who betrayed me. My handmaiden – my dearest friend since childhood, my *only* friend – was murdered before my eyes."

Ian said nothing, but she thought she noticed his face soften just a fraction.

Blair's hand settled on the small of her back. "Susanna..." he said quietly. "Ye do no have to-"

"They tried to rape me, Ian," she continued, her voice rising as her anxiety grew at the retelling of her ordeal, something she'd not spoken of since it had happened. "There were four of them, and they all planned to rape me. They nearly did." She met the gaze of several other men who had fallen silent and were listening intently to her. "They would have, had his Grace not found me when he did. If you do not believe that I love your laird, that is one thing, but I beg you, do not think me so callous as to have no feeling at all for the man who saved my life, not to mention my purity."

There was a long pause as the crowd digested her words. Then one of the drunker fellows attempted to save the group from the awkward reprieve by bellowing, "Aye, saved it, for himself!"

The ribald comment did not have the intended effect. If anything, the men and women grew even quieter. Apparently even a roomful of drunken Scots had their limits, Susanna found herself thinking wryly.

Blair stood and slammed his fist down onto the table in a sudden burst of fury. Susanna shrank away from him, knocking over her wine in the process. "Who said it?" he asked. His voice was so soft it was barely audible even to his bride, less than an arm's length from him. Much like the night when they'd argued, and he'd grown suddenly quiet, Susanna was unnerved by his calm. It was when he grew so tranquil, she realized, that he was truly angry. It wasn't when he was yelling that one should be frightened of him – it was when he stopped.

"Well?" he prompted.

"Yer Grace," a rather portly, older man stood, wobbling on inebriated legs. "I didna mean to-"

"Dougal," Blair cut him off. His jaw ticked. "Get out."

It looked for a moment as if Dougal intended to protest, but then he lowered his head and left the hall without another word.

"His uncle," Ian supplied with a whisper against Susanna's ear. "One of his favorites. That's two he's banished since ye've been here, Duchess."

"And before I arrived?" she asked before she could stop herself.

"None. Do ye take my meanin' now about how he's changed?"

She didn't answer. Yes, she understood, a bit too well, in fact. She knew she invoked something archaic in her husband, just as he did in her. And, if she were honest, she didn't want things any different. When he was dominant, possessive, *primal*, she liked it.

Suddenly, her attention was drawn to a clamorous noise just through the stone archway that led to the kitchen. She heard a woman's voice – a high, desperate wail – and was on her feet within moments. With Blair just behind her, she rushed to the kitchen.

Ruadh stood in the center of the large kitchen. She caught sight of Susanna and ran forth, dropping to her knees and burying her face in Susanna's skirts. "Milady!" she cried.

"Shh," Susanna said, stroking the girl's hair with her hand. "Ruadh, what has happened?"

"He's gone!"

"Who is gone?" Susanna knelt so that she was eye-level with her new friend, who immediately collapsed into her arms, crying.

"I canna find him anywhere, Milady! He is no in the castle, I've searched everywhere!" she sobbed helplessly.

"Ruadh, who can't ye find?" Blair spoke up. He crouched next to the women, one hand on Susanna's shoulder.

Susanna's heart sank. *Oh no, please do not let it be the boy...*

Ruadh lifted her head and regarded them with red-rimmed eyes. "Fergus."

Chapter Twelve

"What do ye mean, gone, lass?" Blair asked.

"Yer Grace, he is'na here!"

"He canna have vanished," he said, but his grip tightened on Susanna's shoulder as testament to the sinking feeling in his gut. Something was wrong.

His wife picked up on the anxiety and covered his hand with her tiny one, giving him a reassuring squeeze. "Of course not," she said matter-of-factly. "He is here somewhere, Ruadh. Perhaps he is playing a game, and hiding from you."

"He hasna done this before, milady," Ruadh sniffed.

"I understand, but things have been rather chaotic the past few days with our wedding. I dare say everyone is acting a little strange," she gave Blair a sideways glance and a coy smile. Images of her bound to his bed flashed through his mind, and he nearly blushed.

"But I told him to stay close!"

"We shall find him," Susanna soothed, her voice low and calming. "And when we do, I am certain you will be first relieved, and then furious."

"Aye, I shall have words with the lad for givin' his mother such a fright," Blair added, but he wasn't convinced, and he knew his brother's paramour wasn't either. Fergus knew better than to run off alone. A hall full of drunken Scots was not so infrequent an occasion at Ruthven Castle as to cause the boy distress.

Beathag materialized in the doorway, with Cook in tow. She gave a slight shake of her head.

Damnation... "Ian!" he bellowed.

"Aye, yer Grace?" The older man was leaning against the wall with his trademark sour expression.

"Gather the men, search the castle. I want groups of three in every room. I shall take a party out to search the grounds." Ian gave a nod in his direction, and left the kitchen. Blair could hear him barking out orders to the other men, attempting to rouse the unconscious. "Susanna, stay here."

"I bloody will not," Susanna stood and took his hand again. "I am coming with you."

He felt his lips curl into a smile. He'd expected her to say as much. But Blair's instincts were rarely wrong, and something felt off to him. He'd never known Fergus to run off, or to hide, and the timing of the disappearance was rather convenient – when the entire clan's senses were dulled from drink and celebration. "I'd rather ye stayed, milady."

"I know. I would rather I go."

"Aye, I know." He passed a hand over his face, rubbed the stubble covering his jaw. "I canna be concerned with keepin' an eye on ye, Susanna, should somethin' be wrong."

"I do not require supervision, my Lord. I can care for myself," she said stiffly.

"I know ye can, liuadhe, but I do no ken what has happened. I need ye to stay with Ruadh an' comfort her."

She opened her mouth to protest, and he grasped her chin with his fingers to shut it. His eyes connected with hers in a silent plea for cooperation. "Susanna, please just do as yer told this once."

She nodded in resignation, green eyes lightening a shade. "All right." She took his hand and kissed his knuckles. "I simply do not like being useless, your Grace."

"Never that, my little English siren." Blair bent his head and kissed her, a light brush of his lips against hers, a small sweep of tongue against her lips, disregarding the fact that they were in the kitchen, being watched very closely by at least a dozen of his people. When he pulled away, she was blushing, the pink flush racing up her throat to settle as a rosy glow in her cheeks. "Men will be searching the castle. See to Ruadh, an' then ye may help search indoors if ye wish."

"Yes, milord." She gave a demure little smile.

Damn her. Whether she actively sought to entice him, or did so inadvertently, his reaction was the same, his groin tightening beneath his mantle. Were it not for a muffled sob from the woman who lay prostrate on the floor, he would have been tempted to throw her over his shoulder and disappear back into his bedchamber for the rest of the afternoon, missing child be damned. *Stop thinkin' with yer cock, ye damn fool, an' pay attention,* he cursed himself silently. Perhaps his brother was right and this 'affliction of love', as Ceallach called it, was a Ruthven trait. Blair shook his head in an attempt to clear his thoughts. He gave his wife a final, lingering caress, and then led his men out of the kitchen into the Great Hall.

"William?"

"Milord?" the boy appeared at his side.

"Ready my horse."

"Aye, milord!" And off he went at his trademark lightening clip.

"Edward," Blair called, searching the crowd for his cousin, as they strode out of the castle en mass. He checked his belt – in his haste to dress that morning, he'd donned his dirk and his sporran, but hadn't bothered with his broadsword.

"Aye, Laird?" Edward pushed his way to the front of the crowd and fell into step with the older man.

"Keep an eye on my wife. Make certain she doesna get herself into trouble."

"But ye told her to stay with the women, yer Grace."

"Aye," he sighed. "Which means she will sneak off as soon as she can manage it."

"She would disobey ye, yer Grace?"

"Every chance she gets." William reappeared with Blair's large, grey steed, and he swung into the saddle. "An' Edward?"

"Aye?"

"Be discreet about it, will ye?"

***

Susanna dutifully followed her husband's orders for as long as she could stand. But it wasn't in her nature to sit and do nothing, particularly while a young boy was missing. Ruadh was a hysterical mess, but she was already surrounded by other women – Beathag, Cook, young Edward's wife, and half a dozen others Susanna didn't know. She felt utterly useless. Cook set about brewing a tea to calm Ruadh's nerves, Beathag was speaking to her in Gaelic, comforting words in low, soothing tones. They didn't notice when she slipped out of the room to join the search.

Susanna moved as stealthily as she was able down the corridor, but her heavy silk skirts rustled no matter how tightly she gripped them. If Blair got angry with her for disobeying his request, well, she knew ways to make it up to him. She blushed at the memory of how she'd spent her morning. She'd never have expected to spend her first day as a married woman tied to a bed. Mary would have positively died if she'd heard the story. "Oh, Mary, I miss you," Susanna sighed aloud.

She heard a familiar brogue growing closer as she neared a junction in the hallway and cursed under her breath when she identified the source. There had to be a few hundred Scots scouring the castle, and which one did she encounter?

"Disobeying orders, Duchess?" Ian asked, coming around the corner with two other men in tow.

"No," she bristled, giving him a pointed glare. "If you recall, I was given permission to help search indoors. Have you found Fergus?"

"Nay, Madame. We've searched the entire castle, he is no here. We are goin' to join the laird on the grounds."

"Search indoors again," she instructed.

"We've searched every-"

She held up a hand and cut him off, repressing a grin at the show of authority which was completely out of character.   Susanna Cavendish, ordering around drunk Scotsmen-- she never would have dreamt it. "I want every room searched again. In fact, search them twice. Do you understand?"

Ian's eyes narrowed. He seemed about to argue with her, and then he sighed. "Aye, Madame." He turned and disappeared the way he'd come, the other men close behind.

"Miserable old cod," Susanna muttered under her breath as she headed in the opposite direction as Ian, down the stairs into the Great Hall. There were still a handful of men passed out on the floor, one had his head resting on the table and was snoring so loudly the flatware surrounding him rattled with each exhalation. She rolled her eyes and crossed the hall, then walked out the castle doors, which stood open. A quick glance around didn't reveal Blair's location to her. It was unlikely that she could join the outdoors search party without him finding out, but the longer she could avoid the scolding, the better.

Unless he chooses to scold me in a certain matter...No, that would not be so terrible, at all.

She looked to the stables; she could see the large, white stallion that was now hers in the farthest stall, grazing from a trough of hay. A lone stable hand was pacing back and forth, a bucket of feed in one hand. She took a deep breath and started towards the low, stone building. She'd retrieve her horse and start searching, though she vowed silently to stay within the castle grounds. Some punishment might be fun, but she knew her husband could be pushed too far.

When she was nearly to the stable entrance, a sharp whinny drew her attention to her left, where a man she didn't recognize was cantering towards her astride a chestnut sorrel steed. She glanced around – from her new vantage point she could see her husband, several hundred paces away, conferring with several other men. Blair gestured to the woods, and two of his companions took off in the direction he'd indicated. She couldn't make out his face from where she stood, but his posture was rigid, back ramrod straight, shoulders back. They hadn't found the boy, and Blair was becoming increasingly agitated.

Susanna glanced back at the approaching stranger – he was of smaller stature than her husband, but had similar facial structure, with the handsomely defined cheeks and strong jaw. His tartan was woven in the same reds, greens, and blues as Blair's. He was a Ruthven. She relaxed a bit and waited for him to address her.

***

Airril approached the English woman with a calm demeanor that belied his inner anxiety. *Ye kin do this. A lass is easy to fool.*

"Yer Grace?"

The Duchess inclined her head and looked in the direction of her husband. "My husband is just there."

"Nay, milady," he said. "Nay, I meant ye."

"I apologize, I do not recall your name." She gave him a demure smile.

"Ye havena met me, yer Grace. Airril, Ruadh's husband." He took a deep breath and added, "Fergus' father." His hand tightened on the reigns he held, the strips of leather biting into his palm. He hoped it didn't sound as forced as it felt, hoped he'd managed to keep the revulsion from his voice.

"Oh," she said again, and her face softened further. "We shall find him, Airril. His Grace has the entire clan out searching."

"He is home, milady. I could hear him cryin'. He willna come to me, I tried, but he asked for ye, milady."

"For me? Why would he ask for me? We should find your wife."

Damn. She wasn't buying it. "He said he wanted me to fetch ye specifically. I am worried that he's hurt, milady."

"What?" her eyes widened. "I shall retrieve my horse and tell the laird, then we shall go find him."

"Nay, yer Grace, there is'na time. Ye must come now. Ride with me."

She hesitated. Her eyes flicked to where Blair sat astride his horse, talking to several other men. "I cannot ride on your horse, sir."

"Yer Grace, *please*."

Her gaze lingered on her husband a moment longer, and then she nodded. "All right."

***

Susanna allowed Airril to pull her up onto his horse in front of him and settled modestly between his thighs. It felt not only uncomfortable to sit in such a way with a man other than her husband – it felt *wrong*. He did nothing improper as they rode at a gallop across the grass towards the woods, did not even attempt to hold her in any way. She clung to the edge of the saddle and leaned in low against the horse's neck, one hand threaded through the animal's coarse, chocolate mane.

She tried to catch Blair's attention as they raced past, but his back was to her, the deep timbre of his voice a mere whisper over the whip of the wind. It would be alright, she rationalized silently. If the boy was injured, she'd send Airril back to the castle for help, and stay with Fergus. She wasn't leaving with a complete stranger, after all, this was the man Blair had picked to marry Ruadh and care for his nephew; surely she was safe with him. Wasn't she?

The journey to the small farm was much shorter than she remembered. Then again, the last time she'd made it, she'd been fuming over Blair's deception and plotting some form of painful vengeance. As soon as the horse came to a halt, Susanna slid ungracefully out of the saddle, and rushed towards the door of small house.

"Fergus?" she called, ducking her head to avoid the thatched roof, which hung low enough to brush the top of her head, even at her height. The interior of the hovel was even smaller than it appeared from the outside, and a crude, mud brick wall divided the space in half, making two rooms. "Fergus, are you here? It is Lady Susanna."

She heard the scurrying of tiny feet in the other room, then the small boy appeared in the doorway, face stained with tears, pausing only a moment before launching himself at her.

"Milady!" he sobbed, burying his face in her skirts, much as his mother had done.

"Fergus, are you hurt?" she cradled his head against her thighs.

"Nay, Lady." His small hands bunched in her skirts and he clung to her as if he expected her to vanish.

"Why did you run from your mother and hide?"

"I didna," Fergus said tearfully. "He wouldna let me leave until ye came, Lady!"

"He?" Susanna gathered him into her arms and hugged him tight to her bosom.

"The man," he sniffed.

"What man, Fergus?"

The door slammed closed at her back, and she heard a plank drop into place, barring her exit.

"Me, Madame."

Her gut convulsed and she whirled around to face the source of the voice – the same voice that haunted her dreams, snaking through her head as Mary's bloodless body tumbled through the endless black of her nightmares. Her mind searched for the vilest word in her vocabulary and when she found it, she spat it at him. "*Fuck!*"

Spencer grinned, his teeth yellow and rotten, smeared with a black, viscous slime. He took a limping step towards her, and she instinctively backed away, her grip on the boy tightening. "I'm afraid that isn't possible, sweet lady. But I do plan to improvise."

Chapter Thirteen

"I dare say, Duchess," Spencer commented, and his grin widened, "yer husband was a fool to think I'd not want revenge against him. And an even bigger fool for not keepin' a closer eye on such a pretty little thing." He took another step towards her, reaching into his belt to withdraw a large dagger. He brandished it at her with obvious relish. "He took somethin' from me, and now I shall take somethin' from him."

"Do you mean to kill me, then?"

"Perhaps...eventually."

"What do you want?" Susanna asked in a choked voice.

"I want a lot of things," he sneered. "But right now, I'd like to make ye scream."

"I seem to recall the last time you attempted to rape me, things did not go very well for you, Spencer."

Spencer's sneer became a scowl. "And perhaps ye forget, Duchess, that yer 'usband permanently prevented me from educatin' ye in that regard. Though I'd not touch ye now that ye've spread yer legs for that bastard, anyway."

"Leave her alone, Spencer," a voice boomed.

Susanna glanced up and saw a large, stocky man stride from the back room. He looked mildly familiar... "Murray," she identified.

"Aye, lass."

"I am bait, then, am I?" She cradled Fergus' small body in her arms. The boy clung to her, arms around her neck, sobbing quietly.

"I avenge my father," he stated flatly.

"Blair has not wronged you," she reasoned. "And he is your own blood, your nephew."

Murray snorted. "His blood is tainted. He is no Murray, he is Ruthven."

"His mother was Murray, and she loved a Ruthven."

"She was forced to marry the Viking pig against her will, lass. Ye know nothin' of our customs an' laws." He crossed his arms over his chest and glared at her.

"I know that she wore this ring until the day she died," Susanna pulled the band from her finger and held it out to him.

The older man snatched it from her and read the inscription, his eyes narrowing. Then he handed the ring back to Susanna, who placed it back onto her finger once more. "This proves nothing. Ruthven kidnapped an' raped my sister."

"You are wrong. She loved him, and she loved her children. What do you think she would say if she knew you were plotting to murder her son?"

Murray's face darkened. He crossed the distance between them with large strides and, grasping hold of her gown, tore a slip of fabric from her sleeve. Susanna shrieked and kicked out at him, but just as quickly he'd backed away from her again. Then he tore a piece from his kilt and wound the two together. "Hamish," he said.

"Aye?" A burly man stepped from the back room.

"Take this to the road," Murray instructed, handing him the fabric. "Put it where Ruthven is sure to find it."

Hamish nodded and approached the door. He rapped his knuckles against the wood three times, and Susanna heard the bar slide away, before the door opened.

"I realize you think very little of me, an English woman, but I give you my word that Blair is an honorable man. And you are making a mistake."

"All Ruthvens are barbarian assassins," Murray argued.

"He is not the one who has lured a woman into the clutches of a murderer and a rapist, to avenge an imagined crime. From what I know of you, milord, you are far more barbaric than my husband."

"I said ye were no to be harmed, Duchess. Have I no jus' proven that?"

She could see a flicker of pain in the older laird's eyes whenever she mentioned his sister. If she could just keep him talking long enough, perhaps she could convince him to let her go. "You have kidnapped me, my Lord. You have done exactly the thing for which you claim to seek revenge. And when you kill Blair, will his clan not seek revenge? And when they have it, will yours not take it in turn? When will it end?"

Murray seemed temporarily at a loss for words. "When yer husband comes for ye, ye shall be let go," he said finally, as if that was all the justification she should require.

"If 'e comes for her at all. 'E's a coward, Murray, I tell ye," Spencer cut in, giving Susanna a wicked glare.

Susanna's laugh was hollow. "My husband is Laird of the Ruthvens. He *will* come for me, but he will not be alone. And then, I promise you will regret this trick you have pulled." *He would not be so daft as to come by himself...would he?*

***

The sinking feeling in Blair's stomach was getting worse. The boy was not on the castle grounds, nor was he in the village. The entire clan had come together and formed a full-scale search, moving in groups of threes. Blair also had the responsibility of overseeing the entire search, and therefore wasn't able to do much searching himself, which made him feel rather useless. He had a steady stream of reports coming back to him, each time his men thoroughly searched an area, and he would send them out farther onto his lands. He'd search the whole damn country if he had to. But, just like boy's mother, Blair knew that Fergus would not run off on his own. He had to be hurt, or worse, for him not to respond to the frenzy.

And, despite the lad's larger than life personality and boisterous enthusiasm, he was just a wee thing, quite easily lost in the vast underbrush and wood of the Ruthven's highland territory. An image of the boy's mangled body flashed through his mind, and he pushed it away.

"Yer Grace!" Edward's frantic shout did nothing to alleviate his worry. His young cousin was running at breakneck speed over the hill towards him, bellowing his name at regular intervals.

Blair pressed his fingers against his eyelids, willing away the dull throb that had started in his temples. "Where is she, then, Edward?" he asked speaking into his palm.

"I...I turned my back but for a moment, yer Grace, an' she was gone."

"Gone *where*?" Christ, now he was missing a wife *and* a nephew?

"I dinna ken, milord. One moment she was walkin' towards the stables, an' the next, she was...gone," he repeated. "I came for ye right away. I'm sorry, milord. I failed ye."

Blair didn't bother scolding the younger man; there would be time for it later. Besides, if he did it now, he'd let his temper get the best of him and do something stupid. Like kill the worthless pain in the arse. With a sharp kick, he spurred his horse forward, heading in the direction of the stables at a gallop.

As he neared them, he could see that his wife's stallion was still in its stall, grazing contentedly, unaware of the chaos.

"Susanna?" he bellowed, dismounting and entering the building at a run. "Susanna!"

"Sire?" The stable boy poked his head out from a stall. "What be the trouble?"

"My wife, she is in trouble," Blair ran a hand through his hair, peering into the closest stall, as if he expected Susanna to be hiding within.

"Oh, nay, yer Grace, the Duchess is fine," the young lad commented.

"Ye've seen her?"

"Oh, aye, no too long ago, milord," he continued mucking the stall, seemingly oblivious to his laird's distress.

"Where did she go?" Blair whirled on the book and grabbed him by the shoulders, giving him a shake.

"I dinna ken exactly, milord!" the boy cried, finally grasping the importance of the information he possessed. "She left wi' Airril!"

Airril? What the hell would she do that for? "Did they ride towards the woods?"

"Aye!"

"What horse did she take?"

"None, milord! She rode wi' him!"

Blair took a deep breath and forced himself to calm down. He ruffled the boy's hair as he released him. "Good job, lad. Thank ye."

It didn't make sense. Why would she ride off with someone she didn't know? He strode back to his horse, where William was waiting for him, out of breath and looking supremely guilty. "She's ridden off with Airril for some reason. Go fetch Ian, an' tell him he is in charge of the search for now."

"Shouldn't ye take someone with ye, yer Grace?"

"Nay, I shall need to speak with my wife alone about her foolishness," Blair said over his shoulder, spurring the horse in the direction of the woods. "Find the boy!"

As he neared the small farm, something just off the path caught his eye, hanging from a nearby branch. He pulled his horse over to the tree for a closer inspection. Reaching out, he pulled it from the limb. The pounding in his head now felt like a herd of cattle running in circles through his skull.

It was a strip of Susanna's gown. Twined with the satin fabric was another, coarser material, in bright green plaid. He knew the pattern, had seen it time and again on the battlefield, had painted it red with his own sword. Blair cursed under his breath and, returning to the path, urged his horse to a gallop. *Please,* he prayed silently as the landscaped blurred, *let her still be alive.*

***

He was coming for her, she knew he was. But with each passing moment that did not end in him breaking down the door, her nerves stretched tighter, and her hysteria increased another fraction. She was sitting in one of the crude, wooden chairs placed haphazardly around the equally crude dining table, still cradling young Fergus in her arms. The boy had fallen fast asleep, no doubt having exhausted himself with his hysterical crying, and guilt-ridden apologies for, as he'd put it, "bring her into such terrible danger". In spite of the grim situation, Susanna could not help but smile at such sophisticated, patrician words coming from the mouth of a four year old peasant child. Blair was right. Had fate – and Ceallach Ruthven, for that matter – been kinder to the boy, he would have made a formidable and competent nobleman.

Spencer remained as close to her as Murray would allow – which at present had him leaning against the table, grinning at her with lecherous abandon, knife gripped loosely in his left hand. Each time he tried to move in on her, however, the Scottish laird would issue a cautionary warning. For that, Susanna was grateful. Without his leash, God only knew what Spencer might do to her.

"Tell me, lady," Murray queried casually from his position against the wall, "what do ye think of our grand country?"

"Until recently, I liked it very much. Unfortunately, recent acquaintances have diminished that opinion." She gave him a fixed glare.

"Until recently, I imagine ye saw much of it from on yer back," Spencer cut in lewdly. For a eunuch, the man seemed obsessed with her newfound womanhood.

She opened her mouth to retort when a shout from outside the door drew her attention.

"Milord, he comes!" a man bellowed.

Susanna's relief was audible, an exhalation of breath that bordered on a whoop of joy. *He came for me*, she thought, fighting the urge to cry.

Murray walked to the window, which was covered with nothing more than a thatched curtain of dried hay. "Alone?"

"Aye, milord, alone."

Damnation! Her heart sank again; just as quickly she was filled again with despair. Blair was strong, but there were at least ten Murrays in the room with her, and who knew how many outside.

Murray shot her a triumphant smile.

A moment later, the pounding cadence of a horse approaching at full-speed echoed through the small hovel, followed by a muffled whinny, then a skid. A thud. More shouting. The heart-stopping clang of metal against metal.

Silence.

Susanna's breath caught on a sob as the moments passed with torturous lethargy. Then, after what seemed an eternity, she heard the scraping of wood as the bolt was removed from the door.

Blair burst into the room, his mantle swirling around his toned thighs, his hair a stringy, sweaty mess, azure eyes vivid with unrestrained fury.

Susanna stood and took a step towards her husband. At the same moment, Spencer lunged around the table and grabbed Susanna, wrapping one filthy arm around her shoulders.

"Put down the brat, milady," the command came, with a fetid puff against her cheek.

Hamish stepped forward and took Fergus from her arms. She bit back a sarcastic comment about the Murrays' sudden concern for the child's welfare.

"Are ye hurt, Susanna?" Blair asked calmly.

"No," she replied.

"But she will be, if ye don't put down the sword," Spencer threatened, and brought the dagger up to Susanna's throat. The blade dinted her flesh and she winced.

"A bit low, even for ye, Murray, to associate with this one," Blair commented with the same deadly tranquility as he dropped his broadsword, letting it clatter and bounce on the tight-packed dirt floor.

"An' a bit low, even for ye, Ruthven, to marry an English whore," Murray countered smoothly.

Blair's jaw clenched. Susanna could hear the click of his teeth as they snapped shut. "If ye harm one hair on her head, I will kill ye, Robert."

"Whether yer woman comes to harm or no depends entirely on ye."

"I will take her place," Blair said, and crossed his arms over his broad chest. "It's me ye want anyway, is it no? I willna fight ye."

Spencer snorted. "I'd like ye to suffer. If ye lost yer pretty little wife, I think ye'd suffer, eh?" He stroked one hand along Susanna's cheek; she squeezed her eyes shut and turned away from his groping. "Perhaps I'll keep 'er after all."

Murray took a step towards them. "That was no our deal, Spencer. We want Ruthven, no the girl."

"Yes, yes," Spencer waved his knife with a sigh. Susanna's gaze traced its movement and she blinked back tears. "After I've paid him my debt, ye may have 'im. But ye said nothin' of this filly."

"The lass goes free," Murray stated flatly.

"Do I have yer word, Murray?"

"Aye." To prove the point, he nodded to Hamish, who had been standing in the doorway like a massive, immovable boulder. The large man nodded in return, and stepped aside.

"Blair, no." Spencer released her and Susanna rushed to her husband, throwing her arms around his neck.

"Get Ian," he told her curtly, and, taking her shoulders, held her at arm's length. "Find Ceallach. My bràthair will care for ye, liuadhe."

"No," she cupped his cheek. "Please, do not do this. Please." She looked to Murray, "Please, my Lord, allow us both to leave."

"Liuadhe." Blair's voice was soft, but firm. "I need ye to go."

"I cannot leave you, Blair," she sobbed.

"Susanna, do ye remember the story of the farmer an' his wife?" he rested his forehead against hers.

"Yes."

"I need ye to gather all the courage in yer heart now. Ceallach will ken what to do. Aye?"

She took a shuddering breath. "Tha gaol agam ort," she whispered.

"Cuirle ma choide," he replied. "Now go."

Susanna gathered the still sleeping Fergus into her arms once more. At the door she hesitated, turned back to face the men. Murray was watching her with concern, Spencer with bland menace, and Blair not at all. His gaze was fixed steadily on the dirt floor at his feet.

"Run now, pretty missy," Spencer leered, interrupting their tender moment with obvious relish, "before I change my mind."

With a final, pained glance, Susanna turned and fled.

Chapter Fourteen

Susanna steered Blair's horse in what she hoped was the way back to Ruthven Castle. Since she had so foolishly arrived at the small farm without her own steed, she'd been forced to commandeer her husband's, and climbing onto the large animal was no small feat, particularly with a sleeping child as her passenger. She'd ended up laying Fergus across the back of the horse, then clambering up herself before gathering him into her arms once again. Several men – Murray guards – had watched her with impassive expressions, making no attempt to either hinder or help her, which, quite frankly, she found rather rude. Although, considering their intent was to torture and murder Blair after her departure, it was probably best that they'd kept their distance. Had she not been so bloody terrified, she would have taken a moment to tell them precisely what she thought of their clan's barbarism.

She spurred the horse faster as she entered the small town of Perth, ignoring the looks of concern and curiosity afforded by the men and women still fervently searching the village for Fergus. Her face was red and mottled from crying, her hair a mess clinging to her sweat-slicked forehead. She should have stopped and gathered the men, but one thought dominated her mind: *Get to the castle. Save Blair.* For once, she would follow her husband's instructions to the letter. Ian could rouse the clan once she'd explained to him the situation. Surely, he would disregard their differences when his laird's well-being was so precariously in danger. And if he refused to cooperate with her, well, that would be a stain on his conscience, not hers. She couldn't worry about the old man's dislike for her at a time like this.

The look in Blair's eyes as he'd told her to go had been disturbing. He had been utterly determined and almost...resigned. It meant either that he had a very solid plan, or he didn't have one at all. Susanna wasn't sure which frightened her more. She should have trusted him, should have listened. But how was she to know that one of his own clansmen would be his Judas, waiting in the wings?

Airril. She hadn't seen the man since he'd led her into the trap. Did Blair know he'd been betrayed? Would the Murrays kill their accomplice, too? Part of her hoped they would. Airril deserved whatever fate decided for him, so long as it was painful.

At long last, the hulking keep of Ruthven Castle came into view over the hill, as comforting as it was foreboding, and quite possibly the most beautiful sight she'd ever beheld.

Beathag was waiting in the courtyard with Edward, wringing her hands. "Yer Grace!" She came running up as Susanna halted the horse. "Ye found him!"

"Someone take Fergus and help me down." She practically shoved the young boy, miraculously still asleep, into the other woman's arms and clambered down from her mount, Edward barely controlling her haphazard descent "Edward, gather the men and bring them to the Great Hall. Now!"

She didn't pause to acknowledge either of them any further. Grasping her dress in her fists, she fled towards the castle, not caring that her skirts were lifted to mid-thigh, displaying her legs for anyone who cared to look, nor was she concerned with the disheveled, tear-stained state of her face and hair.

"But milady," Edward called after her, "Where is the Duke?"

She nearly tripped as she took the steps up to the entrance two at a time, chest heaving from both anxiety and physical exertion. She wasn't used to either. "Ian!" she called, running through the wide, open double doors. "Ian!"

"Yer Grace?"

"Ian, where are the men?"

"Looking fer the boy." He had a tankard of whiskey in his hand.

"Beathag has Fergus. Edward is gathering the men outside, I need everyone here."

"But, milady, why? What has happened?"

"They have him!" she exclaimed. "We have to gather the men and go back."

"Who took who where?" He set his tankard down and crossed his arms over his chest.

"The Murrays and that bastard, Spencer. They have Blair, at Ruadh's farm." She felt a sob rising in her throat. "He traded his life for mine."

Ian seemed stunned to silence; quite possibly for the first time in his life. Edward appeared through the doorway, over a dozen men in tow, who filled the perimeter of the hall.

"We must find Kelly," she continued in a shrill, frantic tone. "Right away! Someone find him!"

"Ye missed me that much, milady?"

Susanna whirled around to face the broad-shouldered figure standing just behind her. "How did you return already?" she shrieked, half in surprise, half in relief.

Ceallach gave her a bemused expression. "What makes ye think I ever left, lass?"

"But-"

He arched an eyebrow and offered her a droll smile. "I thought ye knew me better, dear sister. I do no follow orders verra well."

"So you have been in the castle the entire time?" She wasn't sure if she wanted to embrace him or throttle him.

"Mostly, though I came outside for yer wedding, lass." He took a step forward and bent to whisper in her ear, "Ye looked magnificent, by the way. Should ye desire to drink with me in private again, I'd be verra happy to oblige, milady."

Throttle him, then. She shoved his chest – hard – and he stumbled backwards with a chuckle. "I am in love with your brother," she hissed.

"Aye, an'?"

"How can you be so flippant when they are going to kill him?" Edward put an arm around her in an attempt to comfort her, and perhaps to keep her from striking her brother in law. She twisted free. "Do you hear me? The Murrays are going to *kill my husband*."

"Aye, I heard ye," Ceallach replied. "I thought he was an 'amoral, classless, selfish son of a swine'?"

"He is." She glared at him for a long moment, then turned and strode to the wall where weapons were mounted for both display and easy access. "By the by, Ceallach, I was wrong about one thing – you are just as rude and boorish as he is." She pulled one of the broadswords free from the wall, nearly toppling over backwards from the weight of it. Edward was again at her side, a steadying hand on her waist. This time, she did not push him away. "I love him with my whole heart. And if you will not help me, you bloody horse's ass, I shall go back for him alone."

Ceallach's lips twitched in amusement, a gesture that was so similar to Blair's that Susanna choked back a sob. "Ye wouldna get five paces out the door with that weapon, Susanna."

"Then I shall drag it on the ground behind me." Her chin jutted in defiance.

"Ye'll get yerself killed," he countered.

"I would die for him," she replied flatly.

Someone took the broadsword from her hands, and replaced it with a smaller, lighter blade. She looked down at the dirk in her palm, then up into Ian's weathered face.

"This blade, Duchess, is better suited fer a lady," he stated.

"Even an English wench?" She tried to make her voice light and inconsequential, but failed.

"Ye have Scottish blood in ye, yer Grace, whether ye realize it or no. Ye are too fiery to be pure English," he replied. "An' my laird is lucky to have ye at his side."

Fresh tears threatened. Susanna blinked them back and whispered, "Thank you, Ian."

"The brutes will have more skill wi' a blade than ye, lass, but ye've got an advantage," Kelly broke in, unsheathing his own sword and flipping the blade, testing its weight and range.

"And that is?"

"They will never see ye comin'." He winked. "After all, none of us did."

***

Blair hurt everywhere. He felt pain in areas he hadn't known existed. His upper lip was caked with blood, which had trickled from his sorely swollen nose and a cut below his right eye. He was fairly certain that his left ankle was broken, and guessed several fingers were as well. If his ribs weren't fractured, then he hated to know what *that* would feel like; every breath was like fire igniting in his lungs, and he couldn't prevent a shiver with each exhalation, as his torso constricted. He was dimly aware that every so often he lost consciousness, only to be roused by the pain once more.

Spencer had, indeed, done quite a number on him before Murray had intervened, reminding the Englishman that Blair had been promised to them alive, though apparently his health was not as big a concern. He hadn't fought off the beating – delivered with a large wooden club – for fear that they would change their minds and go after Susanna.

He was thoroughly secured to a chair somewhere in the Murray stronghold, having been removed from the small farm and taken off Ruthven land as soon as the scouts reported Susanna's horse to be out of sight. His feet were bound to the two front legs of the chair, his arms tied behind his back in a manner that was not at all comfortable. His wrists were bound so tightly that the crude rope bit into his flesh and he felt the warm slickness of blood pooling in his curled palms. One of his eyes was swollen shut. The other he held closed, to avoid the sting of the steady stream of sweat that dripped from his forehead.

He also didn't have a plan. He was, as his brother would say, fucked. He was taking the chance that Ceallach had disobeyed his orders and stayed, if not in the castle, in the vicinity of it, possibly with one of his many paramours in Perth. After all, his brother could refuse to help, being angry over his impromptu banishment. And, shoulder Blair die, Ceallach would assume the titles of Duke and Laird.

But the younger Ruthven had never been much interested in the responsibilities of leadership, only in the money that he received, and the endless string of women at his disposal. He'd often stated that, had he been born the eldest, he would have gladly abdicated to Blair.

Blair hadn't had much of a choice, anyway. He couldn't have let Susanna stay, and risk her safety. Robert Murray was a scoundrel and a coward, but he was likely too frightened of the wrath of Henry and the Earl of Devon to harm Susanna. Spencer, however, had no scruples at all. This way, Blair could keep Spencer in his sights, Murray could keep Spencer in line, and Susanna would be safe.

He would die for her, his feisty English wife. And if the bean nighe saw fit to bring him back to life, he'd die for her again if necessary.

Even if Ceallach wasn't in the vicinity, he knew Susanna would likely try to rouse his clan and come after him, foolish, impetuous, disobedient woman that she was. If he waited long enough, he expected he'd hear her lilting contralto, demanding his release. But, for a warrior, waiting was not a plan. Waiting was something one did when one expected to die, and despite the dreariness of the circumstances, not to mention the pain, he was not planning on dying any time soon.

He had far too many things left incomplete to die now. For one, his wife still deserved a scolding for leaving the castle against his instruction, not to mention riding off with a man she'd never met. She deserved to be scolded, and punished, for sure, and he had a feeling she'd only be too willing to accept her penance. Ah, yes, he had much to live for.

Heedless of the tortured state of the rest of his body, his cock stiffened at the thought. It figured that that specific portion of his anatomy would ignore his predicament utterly.

If ye kin get hard, yer still alive, quipped his inner voice, which sounded a lot like his brother at the moment.

The sound of footsteps caused his prick to shrink again, as swiftly as it had risen.

"Ye haven't passed out, have ye?" Spencer's voice cut into his thoughts like a knife. "I though ye assassins were tougher than that."

"I seem to recall beatin' ye to a pulp, English dog," Blair replied, his voice hoarse and strained.

Spencer laughed. "Ye look worse off than I at the moment, Scot."

"Aye, but ye had to tie me up to best me."

"Shut yer mouth," Spencer snapped, and kicked him swiftly in his shin, directly above his already throbbing left ankle.

Blair grunted, but wouldn't give him the satisfaction of crying out. He slitted his good eye open and saw Murray standing off to the side. "Do ye ken what I heard, Robert?" Blair questioned acerbically.

Murray lifted an eyebrow, but said nothing.

"I heard that the reason yer father was so distraught over my mother's choice of husbands, was that he'd been saving her for himself."

The blow was swift, hard, and not unexpected. It snapped his head to the side, and his teeth cut into his cheek, drawing still more blood.

" 'E's tryin' to provoke ye, ye sot," Spencer supplied. "So that ye'll kill 'im swiftly."

"Nay," Murray shook his head. "He has no intention of dyin' today. He's stalling."

"'E banished 'is brother, no help is comin'."

"Aye, but his bràthair rarely listens. Am I right, Ruthven?"

Blair spat blood and flashed a sanguine grin at both men. "I canna remember the last time he did."

Murray snorted. "An' who did he bed this time?"

Another grin, though this one was mirthless. "My wife."

"I knew she was a whore!"

"I'm beginnin' to think, Spencer, that the lass could fuck half o' Scotland an' still have my respect, because she refused the likes o' ye," Murray replied, to Blair's surprise. "I dare say, Ruthven, I like her. Spirited little thing."

Blair's grin widened, the cut in his lip stretching painfully. "Ye've no idea, Murray."

****

"Blàr is goin' to have me flayed when he finds out I let ye come along, lass," Ceallach said with a snort as they rode through the woods towards the Murray stronghold. Ceallach and Ian were in agreement that the kidnappers would have moved Blair to their own territory by now, knowing that they would be at a severe disadvantage if they remained on Ruthven land. They'd set out with nearly a hundred men on horseback, Susanna and Ceallach leading the small, impromptu army, with Ian and Edward just behind.

"Then why did you?"

"Because I am far more afraid of ye than I am of him."

Susanna chuckled. "I have a feeling he will understand. He is accustomed to you disobeying his orders; why I should be any more frustrating is beyond my comprehension."

"Because he loves ye, lass."

"You are his brother, he loves you as well, though granted in a different way."

Ceallach grunted. "I certainly hope so. I've never heard a woman scream as ye did this morn. Ye've brought about somethin' wholly unexpected in my rigid older brother."

She stiffened and shot him a scandalized look. "Must every discussion be carnal with you, brother?"

"It is a favorite subject of mine."

"So the whole of Scotland seems to think. Why is it that you do not care that the entire country views you as a rake and a cad?"

His smile was wolfish – and devilishly handsome. "Why should I care?"

"Because someday, Kelly, you will fall in love yourself, and then you will understand."

They fell into an awkward silence as they rode, spurring their mounts faster; with each passing moment, the chances of finding Blair alive dwindled.

Before long the high tower of the castle came into view, peeking over the hills.

"When we get to the castle, ye are to stay outside."

"I bloody will not," Susanna replied, shooting him an annoyed stare.

"Ye bloody will so, Susanna," Ceallach countered. "We willna be able to simply walk up an' knock on the door. There'll be a fight inside, an' I imagine a damn good one, too."

"Then you will need my help."

He flashed her a smile. "I need ye to stay alive, sweet sister. I have no intention of letting ye die as I save my bràthair, an' I canna keep an eye on ye every moment once the fighting starts. I want ye as far away from it as possible."

She opened her mouth to protest, but he silenced her with a strong hand rather scandalously dropped onto her thigh.

"I'll tie ye to a tree if I have to, milady. An' despite clear evidence otherwise, I promise I am no as susceptible to yer considerable charms as Blàr." As if to contradict himself, he gave her leg a squeeze.

"I am capable of looking after myself," she said with reticence.

"Aye, I've no doubt. But if ye are in the midst of the fray, both Blàr an' I will no be able to help worryin' about ye, an' it could get us both killed. I hope that is'na somethin' ye want to happen."

"No," she admitted, and dropped her gaze. "No, it is not."

"Good.   Edward?" Ceallach called over his shoulder.

"Aye?" The younger man edged his horse forward to ride next to them.

"Pick four other men to stay with the lady, besides yerself. Just to be certain she keeps her word. An' Edward?"

"Aye?"

"Try no to lose her this time, aye?"

Edward flushed and sputtered, "Nay, of course no."

Susanna looked indignantly from one man to the other. "I have given you my word that I would stay put."

"Mmhmm." He held up one fist at his side and slowed his horse to a walk, then a halt. He jerked the reins to one side and swiveled his horse to face Susanna.

Bothwell Castle was growing on the horizon; a much shorter structure than Ruthven Castle, but greater in length. Even from their current position, Susanna could see the line of armed guards flanking the entrance.

"I do not need a chaperone," she continued, though with less enthusiasm, after having seen the enemy. All appeared to be large, beefy men with very large, very deadly looking swords.

"Verra well," Ceallach tipped his head. "Edward?"

"Aye?"

"Stay here so ye do no get hurt, lad."

Edward lifted an eyebrow. "But, Ceallach-"

"Lady Susanna?" Ceallach continued.

"Yes?"

"Stay with the lad an' keep an eye on him, aye? To be certain he follows orders."

Susanna bit her cheeks to prevent a smile. "You are a pain in the arse, brother."

"Aye, so yer husband says." He withdrew his sword with a 'swoosh'. "But this is as far as ye go either way. Remember, ye have a weapon. Use it if ye need to." He nodded at Ian, and swung his horse around once more. Then with a sharp kick, he was galloping towards the ominous stronghold, his weapon gripped tight in his right hand, the hilt resting against his thigh.

The rest of the men thundered past her, each of them drawing their own swords, several emitting sharp, animalistic cries. The Murrays saw them and began to move as well, some rushing inside, others drawing their weapons and running towards the approaching band.

"So," Edward said, shouting to be heard, "lovely day, is it no, milady?"

***

Blair wasn't sure how long it had been since he'd been left alone again. Moments? Days? Not that it mattered. He remained completely still and kept his eyes closed. He would have slept if he'd been able, to keep his strength up. He didn't know how much longer Murray was going to keep him alive, but he knew his wasn't an indefinite stay inside Bothwell Castle, and he was likely on borrowed time as it was.

If ye dally much longer, Ceallach, I'll haunt ye the rest of yer days, he vowed silently.

He felt the fighting before he heard it, the stomp of booted feet, and the clash of metal swords reverberating through his aching bones. His heart responded, matching the rhythm of the clamor, sign of the seasoned warrior even in his incapacitated state. His right hand itched for his blade, heedless of the blood that slicked his palm, and the tingling throb in his fingers.

He tried to stay calm and patient as the battle grew closer, the muffled shouts and dying cries of the men ringing in his ears. This, he concluded with a pained sigh, was worse than the waiting -- to be so close to the fight and unable to join it. His adrenaline had kicked in, the discomfort and pain receding in the wake of that familiar tide of battle lust. The beast within him stirred. The beast was restless.

The beast was angry.

Suddenly the door creaked open. The light in the room was dim – the deeply recessed windows cut into the stone afforded only the barest shimmer of sun – but Blair easily identified the form that filled the doorway.

"About time," he grunted, hiding his relief.

"Come on," Ceallach withdrew his dirk and cut through the ropes around Blair's wrists first, followed by those around his feet. "We havena got much time. Ian canna hold them back forever."

"I'm guessin' ye dinna try the stealthy approach, then?" Blair asked, letting his arms hang limp at his sides and curling his fists tentatively. He breathed a sigh of relief upon discovering that his fingers, though sore and likely sprained, were not broken.

Ceallach snorted. "I've never been the stealthy type, bràthair."

True. Though he'd hoped his clan would try to at least sneak past some of the Murray's forces, with his brother at the head of the offensive, he'd known it wasn't likely. "So, ye disobeyed me an' stayed in the castle?"

"Aye," Ceallach extended his hand. "Aren't ye glad I did?"

Blair reached out and gripped his brother's forearm, laboring to his feet. "Aye, I am."

Ceallach slipped an arm around his torso, supporting him as he limped to the door. "An' ye say I'm worthless..."

"Worthless, nay. But a pain in the arse, to be sure."

"Can ye walk, bràthair?"

"Aye, more or less." Blair tested his weight on each leg. He couldn't stand fully on his left ankle, but on his right, he did fairly well.

"An' kin ye fight?" Cealleach produced his broadsword and offered it.

"That," he took the weapon into his non-dominant hand and tested the weight of the blade, cutting the air, "will no be a problem."

"Good." Ceallach stepped through the doorway. "The fighting is mostly in the Hall and outside. Ian an' Andrew are leading the offensive; I left to find ye. I canna imagine we'll get out of here without a bit more bloodshed."

"Spencer and the laird?"

"We've no found 'em."

"Susanna?"

"She's fine, Blàr. Angry as a wildcat, but fine."

"She's here," he stated. It wasn't a question; he knew his wife well enough. And he was grateful for the knowledge of her presence, for just as the idea of her had kept up his faith as he'd been bound and beaten, so would it spur him to fight with the last bit of strength he had.

"Aye, she is. But outside, away from the fighting."

Blair chuckled. "Ye think so, do ye?"

"She'll no come into the castle, bràthair, I saw to it." Ceallach gave him a sly, sideways glance. "I threatened to tie her to a tree. Although, it seems she's had some pleasurable experiences with being bound, given the way she blushed at the mention of it."

If he'd had the concentration, he would have punched the younger man. He settled instead for a one-eyed glare, which he hoped was at least mildly threatening.

The pair moved down the corridor at a slow, but steady pace, the noise of battle growing as they approached the Great Hall. Blair's muscles tensed and gave his sword another test swing. With a nod to his brother, he turned the corner and joined the fight.

***

"What could possibly be taking so long?" Susanna asked, surveying the castle entrance with an anxious, worried gaze.

"Oh, I dinna ken, milady," one of her escorts replied blandly, "perhaps a battle?"

"Well thank you very much, whatever your name is," she snapped. Had it been hours? Lord, it felt like hours since Ceallach had led the men into the castle and disappeared behind the large, wooden doors. There had been fighting outside, but from what she could tell, the majority of the conflict was occurring inside the castle walls, and she had not been approached, or even noticed, it seemed.

Inexperienced though she was with a blade, Susanna had to admit she was itching for a fight. She was angry. She needed a method with which to channel her rage, and idling at a distance with Edward and his compatriots was doing nothing to ease her mind.

There was also her guilt to contend with. Had she not been so foolish as to ride off with Airril, none of this would have happened. But truly, what choice had she been given? If she'd refused to go, would they have killed Fergus? And wouldn't that have made her feel even more guilty than she did now?

Would Airril really have killed his own son? *Stepson*, she corrected herself. *And yes, it seems he would have.*

"Yer Grace," Edward startled her from her brooding with an outstretched hand, one finger pointing towards the castle, "there."

Following his finger, Susanna saw them – equal in both height and stature, the brothers burst through the entrance doors, Blair with his sword in his left hand, Ceallach with his in his right. She immediately took off at a run in their direction.

"Lady Susanna, no!"

She was halfway up the hill when he finally caught her. "Unhand me!" she shrieked, trying to jerk away from his grasp, but he held her firm around the elbow.

"Nay, milady. Do ye recall what Ceallach said? If ye distract him, ye'll get him killed."

"I need to go to him," she protested.

"Ye need to stay out of harm, Duchess. Ye promised."

Blast. She *had* promised. "I just need to see that he is all right," she confessed finally, giving Edward a pleading look.

"Ye kin see him from here, milady. We go no closer."

She could see him, quite satisfactorily, from this distance, and so, with a resigned nod, she plopped down in the grass, her voluminous skirts billowing around her.

There was something almost...alluring about watching the two men fight; broad, muscled shoulders rippling with each swing of their swords, powerful chests covered in a light sheen of sweat and gore. The brothers cut a swath through their opponents, working in tandem, back to back as they engaged in a powerful, deadly dance. Their movements were coordinated, precise.

They left a trail of dead and dying in their wake, men falling with sharp cries and chilling screams, though she realized that not all of the fallen were Murrays; men bearing the Ruthven tartan also littered the ground.

The longer they fought, however, the more apparent it became that Blair was injured. Susanna realized with horror that not all of the blood smearing his body was that of his opponents – a steady stream running down his left thigh was accompanied by a limp, growing more pronounced with each step. His face was bloodied and bruised, one eye swollen completely shut. Aware of her presence, he'd obviously attempted to shield his wounds from her studious gaze, but as the fighting intensified, he'd been forced to abandon the effort to conceal his right side, twisting in the tide of combat, deflecting the blows that seemed to strike at him from every angle as more men rushed him.

On the other side of the fray, Susanna could make out Ian, fighting with just as much finesse as the brothers. His age was, apparently, not a disadvantage, as he took down men twice his size with deliberate arcs of his blade.

And then she saw him. Astride a gigantic, black horse, broadsword held out to one side, the Murray laird galloped towards Blair from behind. Her husband, engaged in a clash of swords with another man, seemed not to notice.

"Blair!" she screamed, leaping up and taking off at a run. "Blair!"

He thrust his sword forward, burying the hilt into the chest of his opponent and looked at her with one wide, azure eye. "*Susanna, stay back*!" he bellowed.

"Behind you!" she shrieked.

He reacted immediately, pivoting on his right heel, while at the same time dropping to his knees. Murray's blade cut the air, missing the top of Blair's head by mere fractions. Ceallach moved as well, swinging his sword up and around, grazing Murray's shoulder and slicing through the fabric of his mantle.

Murray cursed in Gaelic, and shifted his position. He attempted to redirect his blade towards Ceallach, but overcompensated, and toppled from the horse, his sword falling on the opposite side of the animal, two arms out to brace his fall.

The action didn't go as planned. He hit the ground at an awkward angle, all his weight upon his right arm, which bent inward unnaturally. Susanna could hear the sharp 'snap' as his bone splintered. Murray screamed, a piercing, agonized shriek. As she saw Blair tower over the downed man, his sword held poised to strike, she closed the distance between them.

The lascivious Spencer was also on the ground, held at bay by Ceallach's raised sword, several paces away.

"Blair, no," Susanna stepped in front of him, placing herself between him and the Murray laird. "He has been blinded by the lies and prejudices of his father, much as I was. Much as you were."

Her husband looked unconvinced. "He has waged war against my family for decades, Susanna. He's soiled my father's name, an' that of my mother."

"I do this to honor yer mother, Ruthven," Murray stated.

"My mother married my father by choice!"

"Perhaps she did," Susanna acknowledged with a nod. "Perhaps she did not."

"She loved him."

"I know. But that does not mean she entered the marriage willingly. After all, had I been given a choice, I would not have come to you, milord." She placed a hand on his arm. "But is not to say I do not love you now." Blair's face softened a fraction. "And if you kill him, milord, his clan will rightly seek revenge, just as yours would have, had he succeeded in killing you. Someone must take the first step towards mending this feud. I am asking that it be you."

"We Scots arena known for our leniency, lass," he replied, but she felt his arm relax under her palm, and his sword lowered.

"If not for me, do this for your mother."

The sword dropped completely, and he took a step back. It was clear that she'd made sense to him, but also that he still desired vengeance for his ordeal, as well as hers. Truthfully, so did she.

"But this one," she stated flatly, with a glare at Spencer, "deserves no leniency." And without another word, she plunged her dagger into his chest with a strangled, anguished cry.

Chapter Fifteen

"Well, I dinna expect her to do that," Ceallach commented with a laugh, eyeing Spencer's corpse.

"Nor I," Blair replied. "Lass? Are ye alright?"

She looked at him blankly. "No, I do not believe I am." Her gaze traveled back to body at her feet. "I just...killed him."

"Quite," Ceallach replied, nudging the corpse with one toe.

His wife looked thoroughly distressed; she continued to stare at the dead man with a mixture of horror and shock, as if she wasn't certain he was dead, as if she wasn't certain *she* had killed him. Blair extended one arm and touched her face lightly, before taking her hand and pulling her against his chest. She went willingly into his embrace, heedless of the blood that coated his torso, and now stained her formerly pristine silk gown. He'd buy her a new gown, he thought idly, cradling her against him. For now, he needed to feel her, to know that she was safe.

Her petite fists curled idly against his chest; head resting above his heartbeat, she clung to him as if she, too, sought verification that their ordeal was truly over. "Blair," she whispered, the words muffled by his mantle, so he felt more than heard her.

"Aye, lass." He tightened his embrace.

"I was frightened today."

As was I, he nearly answered. "Ye are safe," he replied instead.

"For now," Ceallach said, "though I wouldna put it past this dog to come after ye again, even after the mercy ye've shown." With that he gave the Murray laird a swift kick below the jaw. The older man flew backwards, back arching as he fell back against the ground with a groan.

"Well now he might, ye ass," Ian commented, with a sharp glare at the younger Ruthven. "Come, we'd best return to our land before they decide we've overstayed our welcome."

Ceallach snorted. "Him an' what army?"

"That one, I imagine," Susanna supplied, one eye peeking out from behind a silky curtain of hair. She inclined her head and the men turned, noticing the group of Murrays that stood a short distance away, arms crossed, prepared to fight, awaiting orders from their chieftain. The Ruthvens had thinned the herd of their enemy, but hadn't wiped them out, and if anything, the waiting men looked angry...and anxious.

Blair nodded. As usual, his wife was infuriatingly correct. "Let's get back to the castle. We kin regale the womenfolk with tales of our victory over supper."

Several men breathed audible sighs of relief at the suggestion, anxious to get back to their wives, and their tankards. Most hurried off to help the injured. Susanna pulled away from Blair enough that they could walk, and instantly he missed the warmth of her

– not to mention the unconscious support she was providing. Despite his efforts, he stumbled.

She was instantly back against him, attempting to bear his weight with her petite frame.

"Kelly," Susanna called, one slender hand covering his heart, her other arm linked under his shoulders, as if to hold him up. "I need help."

"I'm fine, lass," Blair protested.

"The devil you are," she replied. "And if you being covered in blood did not prove it, then you not scolding me for being here certainly does."

"I will." The constant spinning of the world around him was making him dizzy. He barely registered being taken from Susanna's embrace and supported on either side by Ceallach and Ian. "Later."

As if on cue, Edward crested the hill with the horses that had been left behind. Ceallach and Ian helped Blair mount his steed with considerable effort, finally resorting to Ceallach pushing his older brother up by the rear – a scene that would have been comical, under any other circumstances. After Ian and Ceallach had swung into their own saddles, they seemed to remember that with their laird present, they were now one horse short.

"Come on, milady," Ceallach offered his hand to Susanna.

"What the devil do ye think yer doin'?" Blair growled, the spark of possessiveness temporarily overriding the pain.

"Would ye like her to walk home, bràthair?"

"Where is her horse?"

"In the stables," Susanna supplied. "I rode yours here."

He managed to straighten some. "Then ye ride mine back as well."

"Yer bein' a fool, Blàr," Ceallach protested. "Ye canna sit up straight, let alone hold the Duchess with ye."

"I bloody well kin." With a sharp intake of breath, he straightened some more, sending a silent thanks heavenward when he accomplished the action without whimpering. "Come here, Susanna."

"I can ride with Ian or another of the men."

"No," both brothers said at once.

Blair narrowed his eyes. His damn brother wasn't falling in love with her, was he? If so, this really would be the day from hell.

"Let him ride with his woman," Ian stated blandly, clearly annoyed by the delay, and the foolish argument.

"An' everyone says I'm the pain in the arse," Ceallach muttered. Sliding back off his horse, he strode over and hoisted Susanna up into the saddle in front of Blair, who immediately put an arm around her possessively. "Satisfied, *yer Grace*?"

"All considered, verra," Blair responded with as much cheekiness as he could muster. He had to give his brother credit, being a pain in the arse was actually rather fun.

As they began to ride, Susanna scooted forward in the saddle, clearly afraid to rest her weight against him due to his injuries. He, on the other hand, wanted nothing more than to touch her, to find comfort in her presence.

"Ye willna break me if ye touch me, lass," he murmured against her hair, inhaling deeply. She smelled of flowers, mingled with the more earthly odor of sweat, which he somehow found even more alluring than her typical, pristine scent.

"You are already quite broken, husband," she answered.

"I'm fine."

"Lies." Her voice wavered.

It was lies, actually, he acknowledged with a grimace, resting his cheek against hers.

"Blair?"

"Hmm?"

"You smell awful."

Several hours later, having taken a long, hot bath which, though he'd never admit it for fear of seeming feminine, had felt bloody good, Blair was lying in his bed, being tended to by Cook, Beathag, and Susanna. Cook had dressed his wounds and applied an herbal salve to his cuts, Beathag had examined his broken bones, and his wife, for the most part, had supervised the mending with a frantic, inexperienced demeanor that made him love her more than ever. She'd balked at the idea of the two other women helping her disrobe him, but had admitted eventually that she couldn't lift his large frame on her own.

Now only Cook and Susanna remained, the former continuing to fuss over his injuries out of what Blair suspected was mere curiosity, while the latter stood to the side and merely watched him through wide, soft eyes. Her hair was still a mess of fiery red around her sweet, heart-shaped face, full cherry lips pursed into a pout. Her dress prettily disheveled, her breasts quivered each time Cook's prodding caused him to wince, or otherwise provide clues that he was still in quite a bit of pain.

But he quickly discovered that his cock didn't give a damn if every other part of his body was fractured, so long as it could still function. And it could.

It was downright embarrassing to be naked and semi-aroused in front of the woman who had once paddled him for stealing sweetmeats when he was five. He pulled the bed-sheet up a bit higher, hoping that his erection had gone unnoticed.

"It might be best if ye slept in yer own chambers tonight, milady," the woman suggested. "So as no to distract him."

Like hell, Blair thought, and was about to say as much, when Susanna spoke up.

"I shall keep vigil for my husband, Cook," she answered.

The older woman looked from Susanna to Blair, and back again. Finally she sighed. "Vigil only, milady. He is'na well enough for...activities."

Susanna blushed. "Of course not," she managed.

Cook gave them each another sharp glance, then ambled towards the door. "I am serious, ye two," she commented as she left the room. "An' if ye do otherwise, I shall hear it. Heavens knows I do every other time. Yer Grace, stop sniffin' at her like a stallion near a filly in heat, I can see ye through the back o' my head, lad."

Then she was gone.

His wife looked thoroughly mortified at the harsh words. Then, with a prim nod, she sat down in the chair farthest from his bed, folding her hands in her lap, crossing her ankles, clearly intent upon following Cook's instructions to the letter.

Oh, to hell with this...

***

"Come here, liuadhe," Blair ordered. "An' leave yer gown over there, if ye please."

"But you are hurt," she protested, even as her fingers went to the sleeves of her dress and tugged them down.

"Hurt, aye, but no dead, an' I would have to be to no want ye." Susanna's eyes swept along his body and fixed onto his cock, which was already hard and erect against his stomach. He stroked his length several times and arched a brow at her. "See?"

Oh yes, she saw. That now-familiar tingle of anticipation tightened her small nipples, before settling between her legs and dampening her thighs.

"Cook said-"

"I heard the old cow. An' I'll be damned if I'll be this close to ye all night, alone, an' not have ye."

She stood and shuffled over to the bedside, torn between desire and concern, between fulfillment and propriety. "You can barely move," she observed, taking in his chest which was ripe with bruises, the inflamed, angry state of his ankle, and the battered appearance of his face, where one eye was still almost completely swollen shut. She wondered briefly if perhaps something was wrong with her, that she still found him desirable even when he looked half-dead.

He grinned. "At times I forget how innocent ye still are." He took her hand and pulled her closer. "Ye simply sit here," he stroked himself again and lifted his hips in demonstration, "an' I do no have to move at all."

"Oh." After another pause she offered a shy smile. "A wife should always obey her husband, I suppose."

"Aye, she should." He flashed an incredibly sexy, wolfish grin. "I believe I told ye to leave yer clothes o'er there."

Susanna undid the laces of her bodice and slid the gown to the floor, stepping out of it before pulling her chemise over her head.

"O'er there, I said," Blair corrected when she moved to sit on the bed.

Puzzled, she retrieved her garments, and then walked back to the chair, dropping them in a pile on the cushion. She saw out of the corner of her eye that his hand had returned to his prick, fist squeezing the base, the tip sparkling in the dim candlelight with the first pearly drops of desire.

"Do ye realize, Susanna," he commented idly, licking his lips, "that when ye walk, ye sway yer hips in a most enticing manner?"

She blushed. No, she hadn't. It certainly wasn't intentional, as she knew next to nothing about the art of seduction; though, she admitted to herself, she was learning rather quickly. She was, in fact, still adjusting to the idea that she actually *enjoyed* sex; that notion alone was scandalous and still made her feel rather wanton, at times. "May I return now?" she asked. Now was not the time for introspection.

"Please do." Blair's voice had dropped another octave, growing huskier as his arousal increased.

Returning to the bed, she climbed onto his large body and straddled his thighs, carefully placing her hands on his chest. Her fingers lightly traced the patterns of bruises on his torso. "I will be gentle."

"I will no be, lass," he replied, reaching up to caress her full, proud breasts, rolling her nipples between his fingers. "Now bring yer thighs up around my shoulders, I want to taste ye."

"As my lord commands me," she replied, lifting up and repositioning herself above his waiting mouth. His uninjured hand cupped her ass, kneading the soft flesh with firm strokes. She nearly purred with contentment. It felt like a lifetime since they'd made love.

"Christ, lass, I am addicted to the smell of ye," Blair groaned, lips humming against her slick folds.

"Such things you say, my Lord," she chided. Her back arched and she pushed forward to make contact with his waiting tongue.

Susanna's attitude transitioned rapidly from timid to shameless. The longer he teased her with his mouth, the less concerned she found herself over his injuries.

"Oh, yes," she sighed happily when he found her clit and flicked his tongue against it. "Yes, like that."

He chuckled, the rumbling vibrations sending delicious shivers of pleasure through her sex. "Impatient little vixen," he mumbled, but complied with her request, swirling his tongue inside of her wet core a brief moment, before returning his attention to the tiny bud upon which her entire existence seemed focused. The insistent rocking of her hips only added to the delicious friction, and to the sensuous slide of her moist folds along his lips. It was odd to think, as she ground against his face with increasing abandon, that her sexual induction had been only a fortnight ago, and that immediately before that, she'd been sickened by the mere idea of her husband touching her.

Bracing her hands on the headboard, she moved quicker, felt his hands clench her ass harder, and he attacked her clit with a renewed enthusiasm that had her moaning and whimpering. Her body began to tremble, approaching that now-familiar precipice of carnal release. She teetered on the edge for one glorious moment and then her back arched, her muscles clenched, as with a final, loving stroke he sent her world spinning, her climax an explosion of sensation.

Susanna screamed his name, a desperate, frantic cry as she felt a rush of fluid coat her thighs, followed by his silky tongue lapping hungrily at her creamy release. Exhausted and thoroughly sated, she lifted herself away and settled again atop his thighs, loving the feel of his cock nestling in her slick folds, her body tingling with the aftershocks of climax.

Blair pulled her head down to his lips. "Taste yerself," he murmured. "Taste what I do to ye."

Oh, God, she nearly came again at his words alone. She kissed him, sucking his tongue and swallowing the tangy, sweet flavor, rather surprised to find that she liked it. *One of these days,* her conscience warned sternly, *you just may prove too scandalous even for him.*

Suddenly ashamed, she pulled away and wiped at her mouth.

"What's wrong?" he asked.

"You think me scandalous," she whispered. "And wrong."

He arched a brow. "Do I?"

"Do you?" she stroked his cheek.

"There is no shame between us, Susanna, or in what we do. I *want* ye to like what I do to ye. An' I plan to rid ye of this foolish notion as soon as possible, aye?"

"Aye," she repeated with a giggle, her imitation of the Scots accent thoroughly horrible. With a sigh she rested her head against his chest, delivering a gentle kiss to the small nub of his nipple, waiting so enticingly near her mouth.

"We're no finished, love." His hands ghosted down her curves, stopping at the dip of her waist and tightening in implication.

"I know," she replied, sitting up, and allowed him to guide her – gently but resolutely – into position above his waiting cock. She tried to control her descent, but, afraid to place too much pressure on his chest, she slid down his length and sheathed him so quickly that they both gasped.

Her movements were clumsy at first, but she soon fell into a gentle, steady rhythm. Eyes closed, she focused on the sensation of him within her, that slight pulse as she contracted around his length, the delicious slide in and out, the tiny jolts of pleasure that shook her each time he nudged against her womb.

"Good girl," he grunted. "Ride me."

She did, sliding along his length as she moved her hips faster, then faster still. Before long she was grinding against him, breath coming in shallow pants, relief again within reach.

She moaned, low in her throat, and he answered her with a primal sound of his own.

"Touch yerself, lass."

Her face flushed. She couldn't possibly do something so...

"I want to see ye touch yerself," he ordered.

She brought a tentative hand to her right breast, cupping the firm mound. Her thumb brushed over the erect peak and she shivered, then repeated the gesture. She brought her other hand up and offered the same treatment to her left breast, pinching her nipples lightly at first and then with more force. She touched herself the same way that he touched her, pretended that her hands were his hands.

"Good. Now here," Blair instructed, brushing her clit with his index finger.

"I cannot do that," she moaned, back arching.

"Do it," he demanded, delivering a sharp smack to her thigh. "Or I shall no let ye come."

He wouldn't, would he? A glance at his expression confirmed that he would. And she was so bloody close to release, that faint flutter of her inner walls signaled her imminent climax. She trailed one hand down her stomach and covered his, resting at the apex of her sex. Her exploration was tentative at first, grazing the unsheathed bud with light sweeps of her fingers. She shuddered and moaned.

Susanna rubbed herself faster, harder, as she ground against his cock, holding him deep with her. As she began to come, he pushed her hand away and replaced it with his own, giving her clit a sharp, highly effective pinch. She screamed and fell forward, panting against his neck.

Her orgasm triggered his, and with a hot rush of fluid against her womb, he joined her in that elusive state of complete satisfaction, strong arms holding her close, gripping her so tightly that she whimpered.

"Tell me you love me," she whispered.

"Ye know I do, Susanna." He brushed the hair from her forehead.

"Tell me anyway." She did know. But she wanted – needed – to hear it.

"I love ye."

She smiled and ran her lips along his jaw line. "You almost died today," she said quietly, at last voicing what had been troubling her all night.

"Almost doesna count, liuadhe." He reached for her, and pulled her in against his side.

"But I thought I had lost you."

"I feared the same of ye," Blair confessed, giving her shoulder a caress. "But here ye are, an' I much prefer to look to the future, than to lament o'er the past."

"What happens now?" Susanna asked, as she snuggled against him.

"We have dozens of bairns and live happily ever after," he replied. "Does that suit ye?"

"Mmm," she offered her lips for a kiss, "It sounds like heaven."

About the Author

A writer and musician at an early age, Kayleigh Jamison wrote her first novella at the age of seven, and first picked up a violin at eight. By eighteen, she had won several state and regional awards for the performance arts, recognizing her accomplishments in violin, viola, and oboe. Unable to resist the lure of the past, Kayleigh finds herself particularly drawn to certain periods of world history, and has spent extensive time studying Stuart Scotland and Tudor England, most specifically the reign of Mary, Queen of Scots.

With a Bachelors degree in English and Philosophy and a Certification in Legal Studies, Kayleigh spends her days attending law school and her nights immersed in the rich fantasy worlds of her imagination. She also loves to travel, and has spent time in such places as Scotland, Russia, and Peru. She currently lives in northeast Florida, ten miles from the Atlantic Ocean, with her two cats, Angel and Jack.

To stay up to date with Kayleigh's writing, visit her author site at www.kayleighjamison.com

DISCARD-BS

SEP 2 6 2008

Printed in the United States
123139LV00001B/26/P

9 781934 678459